I0544036

Not Really Homeless

Teresa Meyerhoeffer Christensen

(Cover art by Chelsea Christensen Buttars)

Copyright @2018 Teresa Meyerhoeffer Christensen

All rights reserved

First Edition

ISBN- 13: 978-1-7328802-0-7

ISBN- 10: 1-7328802-0-4

Bridge2WorldsBooks
5942 Harvest Point Circle
Mountain Green, Utah 84050

www.teresameyerhoefferchristensen.com

Dedicated to my female family flower chain...
Pauline, Bonnie, Emily, Stephanie, Chelsea, Hailey,
Macey, Lirenza, Halle, Ashley, Karley, Kylie, Aurora
Rose and all future females to join the family.

Books by Teresa Meyerhoeffer Christensen

Seth Row

Angels Unshelved

PROLOGUE:

Poppy pulled her grandmother's flowered quilt tighter around her shoulders with just her nose poking out. She liked to keep one of the car windows cracked slightly open for ventilation, it was going to be a cooler autumn this year. Brrrr. The chill and humidity crept through the thinning threads of the blanket causing her teeth to chatter. She drew her knees up closer to her chin to keep the heat in. Trying to get a little more comfortable, Poppy rolled to her other side, but the rear seat cushions on her 1999 Honda Civic were just not conducive to a five-star sleep anyway which way she turned. Having her spine against the back of the seat was definitely the warmer position.

Sounds from the starless night surrounded her. Stray noises used to stress her out, but now were oddly comforting and homey. She could hear a siren shrieking over the distant traffic. Small creatures of some variety scurried around the tires under her car and occasionally padded across the roof above her. A bonk pinged on the metal roof, likely an errant nut from the squirrels she saw in the trees during the dusk light. It must be too cold for crickets. Poppy started counting backwards from one hundred to take her mind off the sounds and help her fall asleep. She should count squirrels instead of sheep she chuckled.

From inaudible human shouts, she deduced a fight must be breaking out in the nearby park. And a chipmunk was trying to squeeze its way through the inch-open car window. This would be a short-sleep night for sure. It was a good thing ghost stories and bedding down in a cemetery did not freak her out or she would never be able to shut her eyes and sleep here.

At least she was not sleeping out under the stars like some of her friends and her lodging situation was only temporary. Poppy rotated her nighttime residence between several creative locations these days. Tonight, she was in her car that no longer started, but was still able to offer her a watertight trunk to store her few boxes of possessions, a rearview mirror to help keep herself somewhat groomed and the back seat to sleep on about once a week.

Sunny-mobile, named for the sunflower colored paint job, had given up the ghost on one of Poppy's visits to her mother's grave. Poppy did not have the money to fix the car and could not bury it alongside the other residents resting here. Instead she enlisted assistance from a couple of not-too-scary looking guys who had been hanging out in the park that butted up to the cemetery. They had put the car in neutral and helped her roll the vehicle to a denser forested area towards the back of the graveyard to prevent it being towed away. Here Sunny had rested for almost a year now.

The sirens got closer as the commotion in the adjoining property increased in volume. Poppy put her pillow, which from the smell could use a wash, over her head to drown out the noise. She hoped Chet and Bernie weren't involved, but they were seasoned enough to make themselves scarce if there was a problem. She would check on them in the morning. Fifty-nine, fifty-eight, fifty-seven.

A sudden rap on the window startled her as she was beginning to dose off. Poppy hesitantly withdrew her pillow-muffle to find a flashlight shining blindingly into her eyes. When her pupils adjusted enough to make out an image, she saw one of St. Anthony's finest, a uniformed police officer with badge, peering through the fogged back passenger window into her makeshift boudoir.

CHAPTER 1

Definition: Homelessness is the condition of a person or persons lacking "A fixed, regular, and adequate nighttime residence" as defined by The McKinney-Vento Homeless Assistance Act. A homeless person is also defined as an individual without permanent housing who may live on the streets; stay in a shelter, mission, single room occupancy facilities, abandoned building or vehicle; or in any other unstable or non-permanent situation.

Poppy Paisley did not consider herself homeless. She had a permanent address even if she was not allowed to sleep there every night. The fact that the others who dwelt at the same address did not know she considered it her home did not count. Anywhere her Grandma Daisy lived was her home. Being homeless was more mental than physical she decided. Wasn't the baby Jesus considered homeless?

One day a week, or so, Poppy had the closing shift at the St. Anthony Public Library and conveniently just slept on one of the couches provided for the patrons in the reading nook. She made sure to get up early enough that no one ever caught her sleeping there. That would not be good. Her friend Russell might be a bit suspicious, but he was cool.

Other choices of abode these days included frequenting a couple of the local shelters. Poppy did not stay at the same one more than once or twice a month, she did not want to become tagged as a regular. Then occasionally, she would spend a warm night in the park, near a few good friends she had crossed paths with there. Chet and Bernie made park crashing pretty comfortable. She enjoyed their company.

Poppy's favorite place to sleep was always at Greener Pastures Care Center where her grandmother now lived. Not only could she hear her grandma breathing beside her, but sometimes the CNA's even provided a cot for her to sleep on. She was careful to not stay more than one night a week and always made it sound like she was sleeping over more for her grandmother than for herself. The care center was her official address anyway, so although not legally a resident, she considered it the closest space she had to real home. She was just not quite ready to be put-out-to-pasture at Greener Pastures full-time.

Poppy also possessed a punch pass to the YWCA. For thirty dollars she received ten punches or visits. Two or three days a week she was able to get a full shower there and not just a sink sponge bath. She kept her toiletries in a back-pack type purse, so had them on her whenever the opportunity for a quick wash arose. The backpack doubled as a lunch sack. Poppy kept it stocked with her standard diet, fruit and granola bars from the local market. It had been a tricky, but doable, lifestyle since her grandma's dementia made it impossible to leave her alone during the day.

Two years ago, Poppy and her grandma Daisy were living humbly, but very happily in her grandma's apartment next to the train tracks on the west side of town. They had been roommates and best friends since Poppy was nine. G-ma Daisy was the best fill-in parent a girl could have until she did not know who or where she was.

Under her grandmother's guardianship there were always three decent meals a day, regardless the basic nature of the cuisine, that in itself was a wonder. Books, shared stories, games and discussions about each of these activities was common. And best of all, there was actual interest displayed in Poppy's thoughts and her growing world. Living with Grandma Daisy was a safe and inviting place to be, from all of her young girl, preteen, and then teenage, experiences. Until a few years ago, when things in their lives drastically changed.

At first Poppy thought it was just the normal forgetfulness of aging. When it continued to get worse, she finally admitted it was more, but they still got by. Daisy got lost a few times, but always eventually found her way home or was delivered safely by a neighbor. Everyone along Caboose Street knew her grandma. Daisy was an icon in the 'Tooterville' neighborhood, cartoonishly nicknamed for its proximity to train tracks.

Until one day Poppy came home to find G-ma Daisy eating cat food (and they didn't even have a cat). A stove burner behind her grandmother was spouting flames she was oblivious of. Hot orange fingers had already licked a black path across the cupboard above the range. They were lucky the old apartment had not gone up in smoke over G-ma Daisy's head. Who knew how many neighbors would have been trapped as well.

Poppy knew she could no longer leave her grandmother home alone. She checked out some of the state-run care facilities but could not imagine her grandma wasting away in those back holes of despair. Even if Daisy probably wouldn't realize how bad they were, Poppy would.

Poppy finally found Greener Pastures. It was not a top-of-the-line care center, but cheery and clean with kind caregivers. Best of all, they could afford it. Her grandmother's social security check, Grandpa Henry's pension and Poppy's library salary could cover the nearly three thousand dollars a month. There was just not enough money left over to keep the apartment too. Saying goodbye to the rickety old apartment, chocked full of happy memories, was difficult. Now G-ma Daisy lived in a care center for dementia patients and Poppy sort of did too, on the sly.

With the small amount of monthly income left over from the cost of her grandma's facility, Poppy purchased food, a few personal items and YWCA visits. She also received a minimal amount of grant money to continue college, so often stayed after work at the library to work on the two college classes she took online each semester. It was not the life most twenty-three-year-old girls dreamed of, but things could be worse. Poppy was studying to get her Library of Science Degree when her G-ma became too sick to stay alone. Her dreams were simple...she was a Marion-the-Librarian wannabe, ha-ha. She may not be living the whimsical Music Man the musical or movie version existence, but at least Poppy got to visit G-ma Daisy every day. Both of them were safe, or at least surviving.

Poppy pulled open the heavy wooden doors by their large brass handles and slid into the entryway. The medicinal aroma mixed with institutionalized dinner assaulted her nasal passages. The abrasive smell would soon assimilate and not be noticed as she continued down the hallway but would likely linger on her clothes. Even the wildflower bouquet she had picked on the way did not hide the pungent odor, but she held the petals closer to her nose just in case. Familiar caregivers gave her a smile or head nod as she wound through the corridors back to the locked memory care wing.

Almost to room #217, Delta Dawn, as she had been lovingly dubbed from the old 1970's song with the same name, cut off Poppy's path. A petite little woman with wilting gray bun and frantically confused blue eyes pleaded with Poppy.

"Have you seen my Gerald? He is coming to get me and take me home. I cannot find him. I cannot find him." moaned Delta. An old box-style suitcase was clutched tightly in her hand as she looked wildly around her vacant surroundings.

"I have not seen Gerald today Miss Whitely, but I will definitely tell him you are ready to go if I see him," Poppy offered. The nurses had suggested she just go along with the patient's delusions. Trying to point out their fallacy just made them more anxious. Poppy left the work of clarifying reality to the professionals.

"I know he is coming. I got all fixed up pretty. We are getting married you know.'" Miss Whitely, aka Delta Dawn, informed Poppy. Then asked, "Are those flowers for the wedding?"

"Congratulations. You look lovely, I am sure he will be here soon." Poppy comforted as she stepped into her grandma's room with bouquet still intact.

Maybe Poppy should have given the posy to Delta. She knew Gerald would not be coming anytime soon unless he was on an errand from Saint Peter. A CNA on the night shift had shared that Gerald died years ago, just before he and Miss Whitley were to be married. Delta Dawn had never wed and now wandered the halls of Greener Pastures looking for her long lost love. Such a storied tragedy, similar to the song lyrics actually.

Poppy was sure Miss Whitley must have had many good years between the two events, but this was all she had left. No family, no Gerald, just healthcare workers and a few neighbors in rooms near hers, whose memories were not any better than her own, and a battered suitcase packed for a honeymoon that would never happen. Perhaps ignorance was bliss at times.

Daisy Butterfield perked up as Poppy entered the small room which was heavily adorned in pink and purple. Poppy was pretty sure her G-ma did not recognize her, the awareness of who Poppy was only occurred on a rare occasion, but grandmother had always been a social woman and liked company anyway.

"Do I know you? Let me look at you. Such a pretty girl. Do you live here? Are we related?" G-ma Daisy asked the same questions each day and Poppy answered them the same, never annoyed.

"Yes, you know me grandma. It's me Poppy, your granddaughter. I visit every day, but don't really live here. How are you today?"

"Oh, just dandy dear. So many nice young people visit me and bring me things. Did you bring me flowers? Do you work here? Do I know you?"

And round and round the conversation went, never really a beginning or end, but re-answering and reliving the same moments over and over. The distant past was much clearer to Daisy than what was happening in front of her face. Sometimes she thought Poppy was Lilac, Daisy's daughter and Poppy's mother. Then some days she was Tulip to her Grandma. Tulip had been Daisy's twin. It didn't really matter what they talked about or who was her character of the day. Poppy just liked to be near her grandmother, or what was left of her. Daisy's body was still fairly strong, but her mind was on vacation. Poppy wished they could get out of this room and take a real vacation. But there was probably adventure enough in Daisy's mind and in Poppy's revolving place-for-the-night predicament.

Poppy put the flowers in water and asked, "Do you want me to stay here tonight grandma?" Please say yes, she thought as the question came out of her mouth.

"Do you live here? Who are you?" Her grandma asked for the twentieth time. She would get sleepy soon and then Poppy would either crash in the chair next to the sleeping Daisy's bed or take off in search of other quarters for the night.

"This is my address Grandma. And I live here sometimes. We used to have that apartment on Caboose

17

Street. Do you remember?" Poppy was not sure why she bothered, but it made her feel better to talk and try to connect in some way to the lives they led together.

"Toot toot. Was it by the train?'

"Yes, yes, and we walked to the market and got vegetables and flowers almost every day." Just a simple association made Poppy feel like she had hit the jackpot. Flowers helped make the link or connect the dots at times, so Poppy brought them when she could. On their limited budget she had to be creative.

Poppy hailed from seven generations of females named for flowers and there were likely more she did not know of. The oldest daughter in their matriarchal line would not carry on the family name but would become a blossom of some kind forever. Poppy was named for the flower that became a symbol of remembrance of soldiers who died during wartime following the trench warfare which took place in the poppy fields of Flanders during World War I. Vivid blood red petals that looked conjoined surrounding a black stamen was her moniker. Grandma Daisy told her they used to sell artificial poppies and pin them on lapels and collars for Armistice Day.

She would rather be named for the poppy fields in the Wizard of Oz, they only put people to sleep temporarily.

Her name flowed from her father, Sargent Kale Paisley. He had been killed in action during the Desert Storm campaign while she was still in her mother's stomach or more accurately, womb. She was the walking breathing reminder of his sacrifice in the line of duty and named accordingly. What a burden to carry.

Her mother's name was Lilac. The delicate little lavender flowers that formed a whole bush with such a sweet fragrance. Lilac's name became an unfortunate manifestation of her reality as well. Lilacs have one of the shortest bloom times in the flower world and only bloom for three weeks at the beginning of spring. The flower seemed an appropriate name or sentence for her mother's short life.

Then there was Grandma Daisy and her twin sister Tulip who had not lived to adulthood. Daisies are more-hardy than tulips in general. Tulips expire before the end of springtime and daisies live into autumn. Had their names designated their destinies? It was a strange thought, but perhaps.

The twin's mother had been great grandma Pansy, a sweet little flower that grew close to the ground and almost looked like they had faces of their own. Her mother was named Dahlia. Dahlia's mother was named Camellia and

Camellia's mother was Zinnia. All three of those flowers looked similar to Poppy with many tiny petals pressed closely together forming a full and colorful bloom. There was also a Rose and Daffodil along the flower-filled genealogy somewhere. Poppy was not sure she would be able to keep the flower chain growing, but perhaps there was a dormant little Ivy or Violet that would grow to life in her future someday.

There was a pounding knock on the door and Miss Whitley stumbled across the threshold into her grandmother's room.

"Where is he? Is he in here? Are you hiding Gerald? I know you want to steal him from me."

Delta Dawn with suitcase still in hand was accusing her G-ma of taking Gerald. Or perhaps she meant Poppy, after all she was the one who had been carrying the wedding bouquet.

"No, Miss Whitely, Gerald is not in here. Let's go back to your room and look for him there. Maybe he is waiting for you."

Poppy's grandma was nearly asleep, and she should probably not stay here tonight. Delta was not going to let the Gerald thing go and Poppy was a reminder of him now for some reason. She took the little lady by the suitcase-

20

less hand and guided her gently back to her room. Then she let the healthcare professional assigned to these rooms for the night know the situation before exiting the building to find far less green pastures for the night.

CHAPTER 2

Following the Peasant's Revolt in England, constables were authorized under 1383 English Poor Laws to collar vagabonds and force them to show support; if they could not, the penalty was gaol (jail). Vagabonds could be sentenced to the stocks for three days and nights; in 1530, whipping was added. The presumption was that vagabonds were unlicensed beggars. In 1547, a bill was passed that subjected vagrants to some of the more extreme provisions of the criminal law, namely two years servitude and branding with a "V" as the penalty for the first offense and death for the second. Large numbers of vagabonds were among the convicts transported to the American colonies in the 18th century.

The night was unseasonably warm for the middle of spring. Poppy started walking aimlessly before she realized she was wandering towards the park. Her subconscious must have decided to bed down there tonight before she did. She stopped by her foliage-buried car to snag the yoga mat and bedroll, then followed the forested path on to her chosen corner of the park. Chet, Bernie and Obi-Wan Kenobi were already there.

Chet seemed almost too classy and dignified to be living out under the stars in his tweed suit coat and patched corduroy pants. The elderly gentleman had become the closest thing to a father figure that Poppy had ever experienced. Chet was slightly-stooped, but tall with wisdom and a grizzled-gray unshaven face. Waves of longer-length also graying hair, escaped from beneath the fedora on his head and warm hazel eyes looked out from under its brim welcoming her. Hanging out with Chet and Bernie in the park was her home away from home, when she was not at Greener Pastures with her Grandma at least.

Chet had been a big real estate developer in the 1990's and early part of the 21st century when construction was booming. When the housing market crash of 2007-2008 hit, Chet's business went belly up. He lost everything and then some. Not able to face the family he felt he had failed, Chet just took off. It was a better solution than a few of his fellow friends in the industry took…by ending their own lives. They may have avoided embarrassment but left their families with not only the financial mess to face alone but heaped upon it the deep sorrow of devastating loss. Poppy wasn't sure what happened to Chet's family or where they were now. He occasionally spoke of a son he wanted her to meet one day. Chet thought Poppy would be good for him, if he was still single. The homeless matchmaker made her smile.

Chet and Bernie were a couple, but not in the traditional sense. Poppy had yet to figure out what brought the two together. Chester and Bernice had officially met under their current circumstances, after Chet had left his family for the homeless life. There was no pretense between them, just as real a relationship as you can get, with all that either possessed totally exposed for the other to see. They were not married, and Poppy was pretty sure their relationship was platonic, but a companionship of simple necessity had formed. Bernie was a long-timer to homelessness and knew the ropes of Chet's new world. Chet was savvy and intelligent, possessing knowledge that gave Bernie a step up in their sparse environment. Their team-up had worked out well.

Bernie was definitely not from Chet's former social circle. She was a little rough around the edges and dressed in layer upon layer of fading colorful fabrics with various clashing patterns. She wore her whole wardrobe. Poppy was pretty sure Bernie was slightly mentally ill, but she was fun to be around and definitely a survivor. Whereas Chet felt he did not deserve a home, after playing a part in others losing theirs, Bernie just did not like to be tied down to one place or payment. She preferred a simple existence and felt she got by just fine.

Obi-Wan was the furry third in their unlikely trio. The so-homely-it-was-cute, and amazingly-clean-under-the-circumstances, canine mutt was their designated watch dog. At times he added warmth on cooler nights. Poppy had never seen the scrawny beast eat and was not sure what he survived on. Scraps did not seem an option in their barebones world, but they all seemed okay somehow. Poppy truly enjoyed spending time with them and felt protected in an otherwise precarious situation. There was safety in numbers.

"We were just wondering when we would see our Petunia-girl again, weren't we Bern."

Poppy smiled at the comment. Chet always teased Poppy by calling her by a different flower name each time he saw her. Poppy knew he was smart enough to remember her name, so the playfulness made her feel a part of their odd family.

"Yup, we were Flower Child. Glad you could join our star gazing party tonight." Bernie joined.

"Looks like I found clear skies and warm hearts here." Poppy added as she plopped down on her yoga mat. It would have been nice to have a campfire, but warmth from flames was reserved for only especially cold nights.

"To what do we owe this pleasure?" Chet asked with a regal bow. "We are honored to have the flower princess join our humble circle."

"Sort of a rough night at Greener Pastures, so I decided not to stay." Poppy admitted.

"Was your grandmother's mind far away tonight. I have heard nighttime can be difficult. Sundowners I believe?" Chet offered gently.

"No, actually Grandma even remembered our old neighborhood, but her resident neighbor, Delta Dawn, thought I was trying to steal away her fiancé, so I took an early exit."

Bernie began half mumbling, half singing a rendition of Helen Reddy's version of the old song... *"Delta Dawn what's that flower you have on? Could it be a faded rose from days gone by? And did I hear you say he'd be a-meeting you here today to take you to his mansion in the sky...* Well the song got the flower wrong and hanging around that place, where they're all knocking on death's door, or with us for that matter, you could end up in that sky mansion before you know it."

Bernie had an odd catalog of information stored in that head of hers. Poppy was not sure what the aged-by-the-outdoors woman meant by the comments she added after the song lyrics. But Bernie often did not make sense to anyone but herself so Poppy just replied, "Thanks for sharing that melodious and slightly mysterious song Bernice. I think I will be just fine with you two tonight. I'm not heading to any mansion anytime soon unfortunately."

As if on cue to remind Poppy of his presence, Obi-Wan Kenobi came over and snuggled his tail wagging body up next to her. Though she failed to feel much added warmth from the boney dog, his action warmed her heart. She was more comfortable here than in a mansion anyway.

"Yes, never fear, we will take good care of you tonight Miss Marigold," Mr. Chester replied.

The foursome sat in silence for a while just enjoying the stillness of the night. There was something pure and rejuvenating about technology-free nature. The sky was their widescreen television projected overhead. A rare shooting star raced across the celestial screen causing an awed "Aww" to involuntarily erupt from Poppy's mouth.

"Star Wars live in action!" she shrieked.

"Did you make a wish?" Bernie asked. "Shooting stars are good luck you know. They make wishes come true."

Chet, sharing some of his knowledge added, "That legend originated clear back around AD 130-150. A Greek astronomer named Ptolemy wrote that occasionally, out of curiosity or even boredom, the Gods peer down at the earth from between the spheres. Ptolemy said that when this happens, stars sometimes slip out of this gap, flashing towards the earth. Shooting stars are hence an indication that the Gods are now paying attention to whatever you would ask for. So, make your wish count flower girl."

Poppy was not superstitious at all, but she would like to believe there was something or someone up there in the vastness of the heavens, greater than herself, who might care. She had a long shopping list of wishes she could request at this moment. Most had to do with her grandmother or perhaps a permanent place to park each night. Then there was her burning desire to have at least one of her deceased parents brought back to life, but Poppy was pretty sure star wishes did not cross the bounds of life and death. A lump of bitterness choked all those thoughts to the back of her throat. Surprisingly what came out of her mouth was, "I wish…to find my place and help make people happy along the path there."

Was she trying to impress Chet and Bernie? Doubtful. Maybe that truly was her core desire, because it came out before she had time to really think it through. She had not wanted to miss the possible wish window.

"A worthy wish that I would grant if able, even if I am not Ptolemy or a God." Chet chuckled.

"Dang, I wish she'd wished for a banana splits all around, or at least a juicy, thick steak sandwich to share." Bernie muttered, then turning to Poppy. "But you're a nicer girl than I am."

Poppy wondered how Bernie would manage to gnaw through a thick steak sandwich with only one functioning front tooth, the other was jaggedly split in half, but just smiled and said. "Sorry Bernie."

"I doubt you will even need a wish to make that come true. You already bring Bernie and me a dollop of joy each time you drop by Poppy." Chet had called her by her real name, wanting to make sure she knew he was not teasing in any way. "Or maybe your wish has already come true."

"Ha, I have more wishes than one star can handle at this point I am afraid." Poppy didn't want to dwell on all she lacked, when she was sitting with friends who had far less, so she decided to share a story to change the subject.

"I remember my grandma Daisy told me an Indian legend about shooting stars and flowers. One of my great grandmas was married to a man who was part Lakota I guess. Long ago, the legend goes, there was a Lakota village and all the people became quite sick except one young boy who seemed to be immune. The elder medicine man sent this boy up the mountain in search of a plant to cure them.

"The boy was frightened by the task, he didn't know many plants. He asked the medicine man how he would know what plant to bring back. The medicine man told him when he got to the mountain top the plant would revel itself to him.

"So, the boy climbed up the mountain. It took a long time. When he finally arrived, it was dark. The boy couldn't see anything in the darkness. He began to crawl on his hands and knees, but no plant spoke to him. He remembered the medicine man instructing him to pray. The Lakota boy closed his eyes and prayed. He prayed hard for the plants to reveal which one might help his people.

"In the Sky World, the Star People heard the boy's prayers. They took pity on him, but they did not know what to do. The smallest star said they should help him by putting a part of themselves into the plant.

"When the boy opened his eyes, he saw a field of plants glowing in the moonlight. The plants were calling him with their shining lights. The boy knew these must be the ones. He gathered many of them and returned to his people. They made a tea from the plants and all were healed.

"My grandma said the plant he gathered was yarrow. The Native American people call it the shooting star flower because its flower looks like a star and it seems to glow in the moonlight. Yarrow is a healer. My grandma used to make tea from it sometimes too. Anyway, that is what shooting stars remind me of, healing, not wishes. But I sure hope the wishes part is true too and a healing can be the fulfillment of a wish I suppose." Poppy wondered if the myth had bored her friends.

Her companions were quiet. Both were thinking about the story Poppy had shared. Unbeknownst to Poppy, they both had much they wanted to say, but withheld commenting.

"Maybe I should start prayin' to those Star People myself. Don't need yarrow, but I c'n think of a few other things I would like them to light up in my life." Bernie suggested.

Chet added, "We could all use more light, especially on dark nights. I'm a little curious what else Bernie would want lit up in her life, but thanks for our bedtime story Blossom."

With that, they all spread out their bedding and tucked themselves in tight for the night. It took Poppy a long time before she was able to nod off to the world of dreams. She watched the stars blinking down at her all across the night sky. If there were Star People up above, she wished they would hear and answer her prayers one day too, with or without a shooting star.

CHAPTER 3

Homelessness emerged as a national issue in the 1870s. Many homeless people lived in emerging urban cities, such as New York City. In the 20th Century, the Great Depression of the 1930s caused a devastating epidemic of poverty, hunger, and homelessness. There were two million homeless people migrating across the United States.

When Poppy awoke in the morning her sleeping companions had vanished once again without a trace. Homeless know how to disappear.

The sun was still low in the sky, so she had time to drop by the YMCA before her two o'clock-to-close shift at work. She could stay at the library tonight. Poppy hated to have to focus so much on where she was going to sleep each night, but it was a constant nagging reality in her life. She rolled up her blankets in the yoga mat, stowed them away in her trunk and gathered a clean outfit before briskly walking to the Y. She made a mental note that she was going to need a trip to the laundromat before too long. Her supply of clean clothes was dwindling.

Showered clean and spiffily dressed, Poppy's black flats bounded up the library's ten cement steps and through the bubble-glass, double doors. Her shower-steamed, nearly wrinkle free, white blouse was loosely tucked into a black pencil skirt and simple silver studs adorned her earlobes. Thick burnt red auburn tresses were pulled back into a low pony tail that she had tucked into a messy, stylish bun. A light brushing of mascara and lip gloss highlighted her fresh, blemish-free face. No one would guess she slept in the park last night unless they had seen her there and that was not likely.

Poppy inhaled the book-smell as she crossed the threshold into her own microcosm of the world. Old and new printed pages intermingled with cardboard, canvas and leather covers. Technology did not really have a fragrance as far as she knew, but in keeping up with the digital world, they had a computer area as well. Not-as-newly-washed-people-aromas arose from that corner. She loved coming here. Her dream was to run her own book kingdom someday.

Poppy was fully aware that libraries had become dinosaurs, a dying breed, since everything was digital and online these days. All books bequeath knowledge and can take their readers away to another world. But there was something about holding a beloved book in your hands, touching, smelling, communicating with it. The tangibleness of printed pages communicated more to her for some reason. Poppy loved being able to highlight her favorite passages, but only when she owned the copy. This book refuge had enabled her to survive her mother's passing. That was one of the main reasons Poppy had decided to get her Library Science Degree. Eventually she would probably need a master's degree as well. Buildings of books needed to be preserved and she was definitely an advocate in this arena.

Since the existence of written materials, humankind has recognized the need for some type of system to keep growing collections organized. Enter librarians. The profession has come a long way since the earliest libraries, with the Library of Congress currently housing more than one hundred and sixty-two million items on eight hundred and thirty-eight miles worth of bookshelves. Whether working at a small-town public branch, a library housing a special collection of photographs, or a legal library at a law school, librarians can enjoy fascinating careers and are always exposed to interesting people and information. That was what the brochure for her major at the local college had indicated anyway.

Russell rolled around one of the tall shelves of books to welcome her, "Looks like you arrived a mite early wafting a breath of fresh air in your wake." He smiled.

"And will probably stay late too. How are things today Russell?" Poppy greeted her best work buddy.

"Well The Tigress herself is on a rampage. She is determined to have things in perfect order for a board member who will be dropping by this afternoon. Consider yourself warned." Russell retorted.

The Tigress was Russell's not so endearing nickname for their boss Moriah Bengal. She was efficient, tough and was one of those shhhhh-women who gave librarians a bad name, but Poppy respected her and usually got along just fine as long as she stayed on task.

"I will consider myself forewarned and get right to work, thanks Russell."

Today Poppy was scheduled at the circulation desk. She would be checking in and out materials, registering new patrons for library cards, answering their questions and collecting fines. When things got slow she re-shelved returned books. Days usually went fast at the desk working with the public. There were not too many library emergencies. Occasionally she would take in a book that had been damaged and have to deal with discussing the issue and repairing it, but for the most part it was enjoyable work. Even returning an item to functional condition again was meaningful.

Before Russell returned to cataloguing a shipment of recently acquired books, Poppy asked, "Do you know why the board member is dropping by, do you think it will affect us or our jobs?" She could not afford to become income-less.

"Probably just routine, but best to be prepared. We rarely get visits from the royalty." Russell chuckled as he bowed briefly and rolled away.

Russell had worked at St. Anthony's Public Library a few years longer than Poppy and was wonderful about showing her the ropes and keeping her in the loop. He had recently graduated with his master's in library science and tutored her with her college coursework when she needed help. He was in his late twenties, with sandy blonde hair and Caribbean blue eyes (maybe she needed a trip to the beach ha-ha). Russell was handsome in a nerdy way, sometimes shy, always kind and super smart. He looked tall, at least he sat tall. Russell had been in a wheelchair most of his life, but Poppy did not even notice anymore.

He could out maneuver and accomplish more than she could any day of the week, so he was not disabled in the least from Poppy's observations.

But Poppy held Russell, and everyone in her life, at a distance to hide her living situation. She did not need that kind of help or pity. It was just a temporary situation after all. She was surprised it had been over a year already. She would not be transient-living much longer she was sure.

Madam Butterfly vacated her position behind the desk as Poppy arrived. "It has been slow, but steady today", she reported as she grabbed her purse and fluttered away.

Poppy located a butterfly pin on Misty's lapel as she passed by. It was a game she played, like *Where's Waldo*. Everyday Misty wore a butterfly somewhere on her person or in a pattern printed on her fabric. She was an amateur lepidopterist, someone who studies a branch of entomology focusing on moths and butterflies as a hobby. Misty lived alone, and Poppy had heard there was a room in her home dedicated to and filled with butterflies, both alive and deceased. A bit eccentric for sure, but Poppy liked rare breeds of any species and hoped to be invited to check out butterfly-world one day.

"Thanks Misty, have a delightful rest of the day." Poppy called after the butterfly-free back.

The Tigress passed by and Poppy tried to look busy. She picked up a recently returned book about saints and thumbed through the pages checking the condition before putting it in the pile to be re-shelved. She decided to look up who Saint Anthony was before putting it away, since he was the namesake of their town.

Two Saint Anthony's were listed in the table of contents. *Anthony the Abbot* was the patron saint of *basketmakers, gravediggers, butchers, swineherds and motorists.* What a weird combination of skill sets. She needed none of these saint services, besides maybe the motorist part, to get her car running again. There was always the possibility of acquiring a grave digging neighbor and she would pass along the info if that happened. Poppy hoped that *Anthony of Padua* was their city's saint instead. He tended to *those seeking lost items or people, nomadic travelers, and women seeking a husband.* She could call on this guy often.

Moriah Bengal stopped in front of the desk and tapped on it with her fingernails. "Is something fascinating you between those pages Poppy?"

"Yes actually, do you know which Saint Anthony this city is named for?" Poppy asked as she looked up.

"My question was rhetorical. Get to work. If you do not have enough to do I can find you something. Mr. Cohen will be dropping in later today and I would like all areas in tip top shape." Ms. Bengal announced as she spirited away to more important duties with a lemon-sucking look on her face.

"Yes, certainly. I was just returning this stack of books to the shelves. Sorry." Poppy stammered after her.

The day continued on in a more productive way. Poppy crossed paths with Russell as frequently as was reasonable and Moriah Bengal as infrequently as she could. Many books of all sizes, page numbers and genres crossed the desk and she worked on ignoring their tantalizing interiors.

It was nearly five o'clock when C. Jaxon Cohen walked in with no books to return. Poppy had never met the man, but his picture was on their wall with the other board of directors. Something felt oddly familiar about Mr. Cohen in person, probably just the library photo had burned his image into her brain. He looked younger than in his framed rendition and appeared to be not as familiar with the library as a board member perhaps should be. So, Poppy offered, "Can I be of any assistance?"

Jaxon Cohen roused a bit from his preoccupied fog to answer, "Yes please, I am looking for some documents dealing with library property that are ancient enough to not be digitalized. Can you point me in the right direction?"

Poppy had read somewhere that the thing most people notice when experiencing a first encounter are the other person's shoes, but Mr. Cohen's shoes were blocked from view by the circulation desk. So, she was left with upper body from his waist up to make a first impression. The man standing in front of her might be considered attractive, if he eased the serious look on his face. It probably aged him ten years. He had gray-green eyes that looked right past her, definitely not picking up enough details to identify her if she were a bank robber. His shellacked hair was nearly black. Maybe it would not be so dark minus all the hair product. There was a fashionable smattering of stubble on his square jawline and a hint of aftershave emanated from his presence. That was ironic. A heather gray linen jacket fit snuggly on his broad shoulders layered over a pale blue, button-up shirt with no tie and open collar.

"I would start your search in our reference section, possibly under government and legal documents." Poppy indicated a few rows of shelves to her left. "I can escort you there personally if you prefer."

"If I need you I will let you know Miss…"

Poppy glanced down and noticed she had forgotten to put on her name placard today, hopefully Moriah Bengal had not noticed. "Paisley. My name is Poppy Paisley." Ugh, she sounded like a nursery rhyme character who had just jumped out of book from the children's section.

"If I need you Miss Paisley, I will let you know. It is a needle in a haystack search at this point. Thank you."

Jaxon Cohen was quite gentlemanly in an ice-prince sort of way, Poppy mused. She wondered what he needed library legal documents for, but knew the knowledge was none of her business unless he volunteered the information. After about thirty minutes passed, she saw Mr. Cohen depart. He unfortunately did not drop by the desk to fill her in on his findings, or lack of such. She hoped he had been successful with his search, but noticed he left empty-handed. It was too bad he hadn't accessed her research abilities, they were part of the reason she was there.

The rest of the evening Poppy busied herself with a few patrons, chatted with Russell on her break filling him in on the mysterious board member visit and then locked up the library at nine o'clock and turned out the lights. Well, most of them, Poppy left on a few minor bulbs to help her navigate the old stone structure in semi-darkness. She knew the floor plan well, but there was something about pitch blackness that made her uneasy. She dealt with enough unknown in the daylight.

Upstairs were the young adult and children's sections. A cozy reading nook accommodated readers with an over-stuffed sofa, comfy chairs and floor pillows for scheduled story-times. On the main floor were all the adult areas… fiction, non-fiction, biographies, periodicals, reference, etc. She spent the next few hours however not amid the bookshelves, but in the computer-corner working on a paper for her Fundamentals of Cataloging class and studying for an exam in Fundamentals of Metadata.

By midnight the words started to bleed together on the screen and Poppy decided to call it a night. She retrieved the blanket from her employee locker and crept upstairs to claim her bed for the night. The library was drafty, old and echoed, but she still felt safe between its walls. She selected a young adult book for her bedtime story from amid the massive reading opportunities and curled up on the brown plaid, cushy couch with a decorative pillow propped beneath her head.

There were benefits of having many places to lay your head Poppy supposed. Nights were always an adventure and each location had its own treasures to offer. With a roof over her head there were no shooting stars to be seen tonight, and grandma Daisy was not breathing next to her; but here in the St. Anthony Public Library she had an unlimited source of books just like Belle in *Beauty and the Beast*.

CHAPTER 4

In the 1970s, the de-institutionalization of patients from state psychiatric hospitals was a precipitating factor increasing the population of people that are homeless. According to the Substance Abuse and Mental Health Services Administration, 20 to 25% of the homeless population in the United States suffers from some form of severe mental illness. In comparison, only 6% of Americans are severely mentally ill (National Institute of Mental Health, 2009). HIV rates are also up to 9 times higher among the homeless than in comparative samples of the general population.

Poppy had dropped off to sleep somewhere deeply immersed in chapter six and did not awaken until she heard Russell opening the library doors the next morning. Yikes. She was jolted immediately more alert than any alarm clock could have caused. She bolted to her feet, quickly folded her blanket, ran her fingers through tangled hair and smoothed yesterday's clothing the best she could. Then pretended that she had just arrived early, before the library opened, to collect a book she needed for the day as she walked down the stairs.

The look in Russell's empathic eyes let her know he did not buy her charade but wanted to maintain her dignity. She had not explained away the fact she was wearing the same outfit she had on yesterday and this was obviously not a romantic overnight tryst.

"You know you are always welcome to crash at my pad when you have to study late, if that wouldn't be too weird for you. I could even help you with your courses...." Russell was too good of a friend to let her totally get away with a blatant lie, but he did not push her for the truth.

"Oh, Russell, you are the best. I am a bit embarrassed. I studied so late I fell asleep and crashed here. Don't tell Moriah. I won't let it happen again." What Poppy meant was that she would not let Russell catch her sleeping there again. She was pretty sure the lumpy story-time sofa would be her bed on future occasions.

"What time do you work today? Russell quickly changed the subject, not letting the awkwardness linger.

"Today is my only day off this week. I need to visit Grandma and then thought I would go by and see my mom too...well you know what I mean." Poppy fumbled.

"Say hello to both matriarchs for me Poppy and know all is okay here. No worries. We are good and so is the library sleepover. There is enough room here, I wish we could open the doors at night to those who really need shelter. Forget about it and have a fun day my flower-friend." Russell gave Poppy a wink.

Poppy bent over, hugged Russell around the neck and kissed his cheek. "I know I always tell you that you are the best, but I mean it. For real." Warm emotion pulsed through Poppy. She let go and left before Russell could see any tears. When others showed her any kindness, Poppy melted into a puddle. Russell was her modern-day knight in shining armor.

At Greener Pastures Poppy used her handy-dandy backpack for a quick clean up and slipped into slacks. Her grandmother appeared to be fairly lucid this morning and Delta Dawn was nowhere to be seen. Poppy was able to spend a sweet hour holding G-ma Daisy's thin, gnarled, blue-veined hand and listen to possibly fictional stories from the distant past. She was not sure if Grandma knew who she was today, but she at least knew someone who loved her was there and that was enough. Poppy was happy to play the part of a role-shifter and be whomever Daisy needed her to be at the moment.

When she could see her grandmother was fading and needed a nap, Poppy departed and headed towards the cemetery. Nearly once a week she checked in with her mother. She may not be her brother's keeper, but maybe her mother's and grandmother's she supposed. Often her graveside visits were on a Sunday, since the library was open shorter hours, only from noon to six that day. Poppy had been frequenting the memorial park since she was nine. Lilac had become her shrink-in-a-box. Maybe that was too crass of a way to put it, but Poppy did find comfort from somewhere as she spent time at her mother's grave sharing her woes.

Lilac was almost a better mom now than she had been when living. Poppy knew her mother had loved her, but Lilac had not been able to love herself really, so the love she could give was limited. Poppy remembered her mother as always too tired and overwhelmed to play or to take her to the park. There was never food on the table, unless Poppy pulled it from the meagerly stocked fridge or opened a can from the cupboard.

Poppy had seen a prom picture of her mother and father at G-ma Daisy's house. Her father, younger than she was now, had his smiling head cocked at an angle leaning against her mother's. His arm was around a vibrant, full of life, lovely young woman that Poppy barely recognized. The mental picture she carried of her mother was one of Lilac lying on their battered couch with teary eyes. Lilac just relocated the resting place of her supine figure from one spot to another with her death. Here she at least had a view.

In her mother's defense, after Poppy's dad was killed in military combat, Lilac did not really care much about living. She tended to Poppy with what she had left to give, but there was little energy to care for either of them. Lilac took in accounting jobs and worked out of their home when Poppy was really young. The accounts coming in shrank and the flower garden she painted on the interior of all their subsidized-housing walls grew and grew. It was beautiful really, in a twisted jungle-y way. Lilac created her own world of loveliness to deal with the brutal, bleak world that brought her pain. Poppy lived in a mostly motherless, fantasy flower garden even before her mom died.

On the day of Lilac's death, Poppy had tried to wake her mother for most of the day before finally going to seek help. Their wild flower walls and her mother's wasted-away, tiny body told much of the story to the stranger who came in to offer assistance. It was obviously too late. Officially Lilac died of anorexia or lack of nutrition and depression. She just never woke up after falling asleep on the couch. Lilac's heart gave out, her emaciated body cannibalized its own muscle.

As a young girl Poppy could not understand why her mother did not eat, when she herself was always hungry. Poppy was forever trying to feed her skin and bones mother with anything she could find. Now with the perspective of age, Poppy realized the cause of death on the certificate was medical science's way of explaining how her mother passed away. Poppy knew now the official diagnosis should have been she died of a broken heart.

Poppy dropped down on the ground next to the simple marker. With both hands she brushed back the tall grass to read the words chiseled into the cement block:

Lilac Butterfield Paisley

May 17, 1977 - October 16, 2006

The name and dates with a dash between did not seem enough to memorialize her mother's short life. Maybe one day she would have a real headstone made, one that stood up and could not be buried in the grass that grew over her mother. She laid the lilac bunch she had picked on the way next to their namesake and said hello.

"Hey Mom. How are things? Hope you get to hang out with dad lots. I wonder if you ever cross paths with any of your flower ancestors? Are you painting bouquets and gardens of flowers on the clouds these days? I sure miss you. Grandma is here, in body anyway, not always all of her. Just not sure where I really belong these days…

I know people are supposed to bloom where they are planted, but I am having trouble finding where to sink my roots. I am more like a potted plant being moved from place to place without a wheelbarrow."

Poppy sat in silence for a while. Not really expecting her mom to reply but hoping some answer might fall from the bright star-hidden sky. When nothing happened, she rambled on.

"Work is pretty good. My friend Russell is amazing. He said to say hello. I think you would like him. I could probably move in with him if I made the right moves. But that would not really be fair to him, he might get the wrong idea about us and I would feel I was using him. Another co-worker, Misty, lives with butterflies. I bet she would love it if you painted flowers on her walls for them to land on. My boss's nickname is The Tigress, if that gives you any insights. She is often on the hunt and I work hard to avoid being her prey. Ha-ha. I do like my job, mostly."

Poppy picked a wide blade of grass and stretched it tautly between her two thumbs, then blew through the slightly open space created in their junction. A shrill whistling sound sang forth from her fingers via the vibrating blade. Not really a duck call, but in that family of sounds. She hung her head back with face skyward and let the sun warm her for several minutes. She should probably be more stressed by her current situation than she was. For some reason she knew things would eventually be okay and she was just trying to exist day by day in the meantime. There were rare moments when she wanted to unleash and rage at the world, but Poppy was able to suck them in. Maybe one day she would explode.

"Well, love you mom. Wish I had more time with you here, not here here, but before you left. Grandma is great though, I can't complain. I guess I could, but I won't."

Poppy pulled herself up off the grassy mound to go gather her clothes that needed washing from Sunny-mobile. She caught sight of Chet and Bernie with Obi-wan out of the corner of her eye. They must have wandered outside of their usual stomping grounds. When she turned to wave they had already moved on. What an unlikely trio, but they made it work. That was what Poppy was doing.

Making what she was given work. So far so good. Maybe tonight would be a Greener Pastures night.

CHAPTER 5

The number of homeless people grew in the 1980s, as housing and social services decreased. After many years of advocacy and numerous revisions, President Ronald Reagan signed into law the McKinney-Vento Homeless Assistance Act in 1987. This remains the only piece of federal legislation that allocates funding to the direct service of homeless people. Interestingly, there are five times more vacant houses in the United States today than the number of homeless people.

Xavier Max was a legend at the library. He was their only patron who had been granted bi-monthly, personal door to door delivery of requested books. This special service was allowed for him partly due to his generous annual donation to the library. The story Poppy heard was that Xavier grew up in a wealthy family as a trust fund son, so had no need to work. He became obsessively addicted to online video gaming as a teen and the habit carried on into adulthood. Xavier pretty much had a gamer control in his hand 24/7 for years.

Mr. Max was known to spend up to twenty hours a day in his darkened den connected to gaming systems all over the world. His handle or online moniker was "Professor X" after Professor Charles Xavier, a fictional character appearing in American comic books published by Marvel Comics. Charles Xavier was the genius founder and leader of the X-Men. Xavier Max liked to consider himself an online genius and leader in his realm of avid gamers.

When St. Anthony's Xavier turned thirty-eight his health had deteriorated to the point his doctor told him that gaming was going to kill him. Xavier was a rotund, nearing middle-aged man, weighing nearly five hundred pounds with all the ailments that accompany morbid obesity. Upon hearing the doom's day prognosis, Professor X quit the gaming world cold turkey. But he needed another hobby to fill his time and Xavier Max was not exactly the athletic type. He became a voracious reader. Albeit another sedentary activity, it was a start. The library staff took turns delivering Mr. Max's reading list and today was Poppy's turn to drop by after her shift was over.

It looked as if Xavier Max was working his way through the classic best novels of all time, or if not, trying to reinvent himself. Poppy stacked the new books he requested in a book bag to take with her on the bus. *The Scarlet Pimpernel,* a swashbuckling personal favorite of hers, was stacked on top of *Of Mice and Men* by Steinbeck, *Frankenstein* by Shelly, The *Call of the Wild* by London, Don *Quixote* by De Cervantes and *The Count of Monte Cristo* by Alexandre Dumas.

A stern Moriah Bengal was standing in front of Poppy as she looked up from her book revelry, "I have an assignment for you Miss Paisley."

"Yes, I heard and am on it. In fact, I'm almost done fulfilling Mr. Max's checkout list at this very moment." Poppy answered.

"Thank you. Yes, that is also your assignment, but I have another one as well. Let's hope you can multitask shall we. Mr. Jaxon Cohen from the Library's Board of Directors called and requested that you search through our resources for some documents he needs. He mentioned that you had helped him on this project at a prior visit and he is not having much success on his own."

"I was really no help, I just pointed him in the right direction." Poppy admitted.

"Well, perhaps you merely looked like you had extra time on your hands. Anyhow, he is faxing over an outline of the items he needs. I expect you to give it your best effort. Even above your best effort if possible. Please ask Russell if you need any help." And with that Moriah Bengal was gone again. She must have more to do than Poppy was aware of, the woman was always in a hurry. At least she liked to make everyone feel like she was off to more important things.

Assignments were merely more opportunities. Right? Poppy sighed. She went to the fax machine and lifted off a sheet of paper from C. J. Cohen Construction & Property Development. The memo was short, but specific. Jaxon Cohen was enlisting Poppy to look for any legal documents that had any information about the library property at their current location or if there were any outlying parcels for future development. Specifically, if there was a section of the city park that was set aside for an annex of the library. He recalled rumors of such in existence but had been unable to locate the legal paperwork he needed.

This was a little concerning. Red flags waved in front of Poppy's eyes. Was the savvy businessman trying to seduce away library property for his own interests? Maybe that is why he selected an underling to do his dirty work? Poppy was not only disappointed, but annoyed if so. Or had she just read too many mystery thrillers and jumped to conclusions? She needed to run this by Russell. He was less emotionally based and usually saw things clearly.

It took only moments to locate her library cohort. "Hey, Russell, do you know anything about library property documents or why Jaxon Cohen may be interested in them?" The words poured out of Poppy's mouth as she handed over the fax for Russell to see.

Sensing slight hostility wafting off of his co-worker Russell began with, "Let's not jump to any conclusions. One thing at a time. Let me take a look. For what it's worth, I have heard Mr. Cohen is a decent guy and fair businessman."

"I am just wondering why he would ask for me, the newbie, to help him out." Poppy admitted.

Russell had several ideas why a man would ask for Poppy's assistance. There was nothing not to like about Poppy. In fact, he was feeling a twinge of jealousy in the board member's interest. But all he replied was, "Poppy you are a charming, intelligent woman. Why would he not ask for you? But I will lend any expertise I can to the mission. If any old legal papers are entombed in this literary castle, we will uncover them."

"Thanks Russell. Sorry I went from zero to full throttle conspiracy theory in under sixty seconds. I will take it one step at a time and do my job. Which currently is to deliver another big-wig his books. Guess I better get going."

"Dropping books by Xavier's is an adventure to another world my friend. He is definitely better than most any character you would read in a book. Soak it all in. Say hello to the big guy for me if you get in." Russell sent Poppy off with a salute.

The bus ride through the east side of town was uneventful. Poppy got off on the corner of Livingston and Lincoln. She could see the Max mini-mansion surrounded by six-foot wrought iron fencing just down Lincoln Street. The structure was not ginormous, but larger than anyplace she had ever, or likely would ever, live. The classically elegant home had distinctive Victorian mixed with Tutor architectural influences and was covered in variegated brick with a clay shingle roof. The tall gates on the sidewalk that opened to access the driveway had been left open. They must be expecting her delivery. However, when she arrived at the front porch, the book bag was not resting in its usual spot on the bottom stair, so Poppy proceeded up.

At the top of the four stone steps, Poppy rapped on the large wooden plank door with an ornate knocker. There was a small window near the top, overlaid with iron grillwork, that was unfortunately too high for her to peek in. Expecting to just leave the bundle on the porch as she had in the past, she was surprised to hear a muffled voice hollering for her to please come in.

She pressed down the thumb lever on the ancient door handle and slowly swung open the heavy door. The entryway had an extremely high ceiling with a chandelier hovering probably eight feet over her head. A hallway several feet in front of her crossed perpendicular to the entrance leading in both directions to who knows where and a wide staircase disappeared upward straight ahead. Across from her on either side, Poppy could see into two very different rooms, each was entered through paneled glass double-doors framed with rich dark wood.

The room to the left appeared as if a video game nightmare had exploded spewing its contents into a dark cave. In-spite of the fact that there was minimal light present with blackout blinds drawn, Poppy could see that every wall, and even the ceiling, was covered with memorabilia. All the greats were represented. She spied Donkey Kong, Zelda, Mario Brothers, etc., etc. There was an oddly artistic feel to the animated decor, but the room's ambiance definitely cried busyness personified.

On the opposite side was a space diametrically opposed in every way. It was tastefully simplistic with pristine large windows overlooking the manicured estate out two directions. Xavier Max definitely had hired yard care or a full-time gardener. Classic paintings in muted pastel colors adorned the walls, the colors spilled onto floor and furniture with a huge overstuffed leather recliner resting next to a bookcase. A peaceful feeling emanated from the opening on the right.

A small glass-fronted fridge full of fruits, veggies and assorted healthy snacks mocked the corpulent man sitting in the corner with crumbs and jelly smeared around his mouth. He sat snuggly wedged in the leather chair across the room. A box of donuts, nearly consumed, was on the lamp table next to the chair. "Old habits obviously die hard. I am reading a police thriller and Krispy Kreme delivers." Xavier Max offered the explanation before Poppy had time to inquire. "Please come in. I haven't had time to put out the books for return and I noticed through the window that you were not Russell. I really need to get a ramp for him and be a bit more politically correct with accessibility needs I suppose."

Poppy startled by the sudden entry invitation and non-introduction merely replied, "I have your new books."

"Yes, yes, thank you young lady. Just put them down and trade for this other bag I have here, if you would. That way I do not even have to get up out of my comfortable chair." Mr. Max suggested.

Poppy was beginning to warm up her vocal cords. "I would be happy to sir, but may I ask why you chose to be inside on this beautiful day and not out enjoying your amazing property?" She knew it was bold, but better than saying, "you are extremely overweight and could use the exercise."

"I do roam out there at times. Much more now that I can actually see nature calling me outside these window panes. I am sure you have heard tell of my infamous gaming days. At least reading is not as addicting, I can occasionally put down a book and venture out. I'm not really ready for a marathon yet as you can see." Xavier wiped his bulbous fingers across his messy mouth, then pulled back his lips from his teeth and gave Poppy a chubby cheeked smile.

"Well, someday you will have to give me the grand tour. This place looks amazing. I am glad you are now opening your mind, as well as stimulating it, with good literature." Then for some unknown reason she decided to add, "Have you ever considered trying to write a book yourself?"

Xavier Max chuckled and the rolls of flesh that encased him vibrated from his chin to his knees. "Now that might be entertaining to a very few and not sure what I would write about."

"I bet you would be killer in the sci-fi genre since you lived in the video game world for so long." Poppy suggested.

"Well now, that is an idea. I could create my own reality and really never have to go anywhere." Xavier joked.

"Not really. I think authors usually feel compelled to go research the things they are writing about. Just a random thought, sorry." Poppy picked up the other book bag and turned to leave.

"No please don't apologize. That is an interesting idea, perhaps I may even pursue it. Wait and let me walk you to the door." Xavier, attempting to be a gentleman, began rocking his massive body weight back and forth until the momentum helped him propel himself up and out of the recliner.

Poppy wanted to say that she could let herself out, but decided any movement was good for the man and let him waddle her to the door. "Thank you. We at the library will look forward to your next list of books and will bring them by in two weeks." We at the library? Whoa that was weird, was she now their official representative?

"I hope I get to see you again soon my dear, as well as meet the new fictitious characters you bring along between book pages." Beads of sweat from exertion moistened Xavier Max's upper lip as he put out his thick hand to shake goodbye. Poppy's fingers were immediately engulfed by his sweaty paw. Many people might be repulsed, but Poppy made a conscious effort to appreciate the friendly gesture and ignore the wetness. She eventually slid her palm loose and waved goodbye with a sincere smile.

Xavier Max could be an interesting acquaintance she supposed. The handshake had not been her favorite part of the exchange, but she decided the man could probably use some human contact. She wondered if he and Misty would hit it off. Maybe she should see if Moriah might send Misty next time. They could talk about their collections.

It was too far to walk back to the library, cemetery or Greener Pastures this late in the day. So, Poppy waited for the bus at Lincoln and Livingston again to begin her journey back towards the more-humble Tootersville livers across town. Her departing glance at the Max mansion filled her soul with the irony of the situation. Xavier Max lived in a huge home with far too many rooms for him to use. Poppy would guess he rarely, if ever, made it up the stairs to the upper level. While she, herself, did not even have one room to call her own, unless a car counted. Xavier Max would probably never notice if she decided to squat on the second story. He would likely just think his home had become haunted. It was a thought, but one a sane person certainly mustn't entertain.

CHAPTER 6

Causes of homelessness in the United States
include lack of affordable housing,
divorce, lawful eviction, negative cash
flow, post-traumatic stress disorder,
foreclosure, fire, natural disasters
(hurricane, earthquake, or flood), mental
illness, physical disability, having no
family or supportive relatives, substance
abuse, lack of needed services, elimination
of pensions and unemployment entitlements,
no or inadequate income sources (such as
Social Security, stock dividends, or
annuity), poverty (no net worth), gambling,
unemployment, and low-paying jobs.
Homelessness in the United States affects
many segments of the population, including
families, children, domestic violence
victims, ex-convicts, veterans, and the
aged. California accounts for 20% of the
homeless population in the United States.
California, New York, Florida, Texas, and
Massachusetts account for half of the
homeless population in the US.

The bus pulled up at the St. Anthony city park bus
stop and Poppy hopped off. She could see Chet and Bernie
parked over on their usual bench and decided to swing by
for a quick check in. She did not have anything to offer

them but her company, yet somehow, they always made her feel like that was enough and a grand gesture.

The two were wearing the same clothing they always wore and seemed quite content. They greeted her with a cheery random flower name welcome, then asked how she was doing. Inquiring in a way that made her feel like they were sincerely interested. Poppy shared an abridged version of her last few uneventful days, finishing up with her visit to Xavier Max's home. Although she had never said out loud that she did not currently have a residence, Poppy could tell Chet and Bernice knew without her having to say it.

"Somehow it does not seem quite right that one man, although he is a very massive man, has all that space to himself when others do not even have any roof over their heads." She was thinking of the couple and canine seated before her when she uttered those words.

"Dear Petunia, one thing my father taught me is that life is not fair, and we are setting ourselves up for disappointment if we think otherwise." Chet shared.

"But don't you think things in the world should be a little more balanced?" Poppy asked.

"Maybe we could get a group together and storm the mansion for possession. If he is a single man like you say, wouldn't be too hard to all force our way in." Bernice in a fighting mood suggested with gusto.

"No, I am not suggesting a riot or insurgency, but there has to be a better way." Poppy offered.

"In my former life I had far too much, or maybe better put, much more than I needed. It would have served me better to have shared some of my property with families who needed it and taken a smaller place for myself. Now I have nothing to share." Chet lamented.

"You mean like communism or socialism?" Poppy asked. "Having all property in common which is shared by the masses?"

"Not really. Communism is not in actuality what it sounds like in philosophy. There are still some in that system who have very much and others who have virtually nothing. I am talking about a higher level of humanity. I am not sure it is even possible in today's world to have a society where people take only what they need and share the rest with others. A world where all work for the common good of their fellow man. The closest thing in this sphere would probably be the hippie communes from the 60s, but I fear their altruistic achievements may have been largely drug aided." Chet chuckled.

"You should run for office Chet." Poppy encouraged. "You would have my vote for sure."

"You'd get my vote and Obi-wan's too, Chester, if either of us could vote. You have been great to us and people here in this park could use some dang good representation." Bernie added.

"I do not think that is in the cards for me at this junction in my life." Chet admitted. "But I wish I could do more good for displaced people."

"You two always make my life more interesting. Is there anything I could do for either of you?" Poppy asked.

"That's not how it works…" Bernice stopped when Chet gave her an unexplained look. He continued, "We are all here to help one another the best we can. Let's not get too serious, just enjoy each day whatever it may bring, our Lily of this valley."

Poppy was not sure how all their conversations seemed to find their way into much deeper topics, than mere frivolous talk. Maybe because everything was stripped down and real in their lives and idle chatter was a waste of time? It was funny that the wisest philosopher she knew lived on a park bench. It would be nice to have someone like Chet in local politics.

"Always a treat to cross paths with you two. If you ever do need anything just let me know. Even a library book to help pass the time." Poppy picked up the almost forgotten book bag and bid them farewell. Tonight, was not a park night, just a layover on her way to Greener Pastures. Obi-Wan Kenobi followed Poppy. It was comforting to have a guard dog in this area of park. Since it would be ridiculously unfeasible to maintain a pet in the transient existence she lived, Chet and Bernie were generous to share their beast with her.

After a brief pitstop at her immobile automobile and a farewell rubdown for Obi-Wan, Poppy went to see her grandmother. She felt more at home at Greener Pastures than she did anywhere else, which wasn't saying much.

Upon arrival Poppy was pulled into the office. A sick feeling crept into her stomach. They knew. Somehow, they had found out that she was using their facility as a home base and were going to kick her out or even worse, her grandmother. Director Metcalfe entered the office and sat behind the desk across from Poppy with a somber look on his face. Should she confess before he could accuse her? Would he go easier on her and let G-ma Daisy stay?

"I have some difficult news to share Miss Paisley. I am sorry. As you know we do our best to serve our clients in all areas... physically, mentally and socially. Your grandmother came to us with acute dementia, most likely Alzheimer's, but a positive diagnosis can only be determined post-mortally. Recently her physical health has begun to deteriorate as well. Her kidney output has decreased, and her heart has developed an arrhythmia. Neither of these conditions are fatal at this time, but I wanted to warn you they are prone to progression. I believe your grandmother is at the beginning of a downhill spiral. We will continue to do all we can for her for as long as she is here. It could be weeks, months, but not more than a year I would guess."

Poppy sat quietly, not saying a word. She feared if she spoke, she would lose it and totally break down. She sucked in a deep breath, and eked out a soft, "thank you for letting me know", as she dashed from the office. She should have asked the director a few more specific questions, but medical science was often a guessing game anyway. She knew her grandma was partially gone already, but she was not ready to have her finish the full exit. G-ma Daisy was her touchstone.

Poppy pushed open #217. She was definitely staying tonight. A nurse with a name tag "Mona" on her scrub top was washing her grandma up for dinner.

"Mona, could I get a cot for the night? I just received some tough news about my grandmother's health and I would like to stay with her tonight if possible."

"Of course, darlin'. I will take care of that right after I get all the girls their dinner. Since you are going to be here, you are welcome to feed Ms. Daisy if you would like."

"It would be my pleasure." Poppy washed her hands and pulled up a chair to the bedside.

Mona returned with a tray laden with a soft food diet and set it in front of Grandma Daisy, then immediately left to tend to the others. Poppy slowly spooned the mashed potatoes and applesauce into her grandma's mouth. "Grandma, I am not ready for you to go. Please take your time. I still need you around."

"Am I going somewhere? Where am I going? Are you taking me on a trip? Am I going home?" Daisy asked between mouthfuls. She was confused, and it was Poppy's fault. Just because she did not understand, did not mean grandma could not hear.

"No, actually I am visiting you right here for the night. We are having a girl's night. So, if there is anything you would like to do just let me know. Maybe we can look through your picture book later?"

The photo album was G-ma Daisy's favorite possession and occasionally unlocked a sliver of her slim memory. "Don't fret about going anywhere, we are here safe and sound for the night."

Miss Whitely popped her head through the door. Perhaps she heard mention of a girl's night. "I was wondering if my Gerald had arrived yet. Have you seen him?" She was in her Delta Dawn attire, wearing an aged, cream color long dress. Maybe she was looking for her bachelorette party.

"Nope, just us girls in here, but if he shows up we will direct him your way Miss Whitely. Good luck." Poppy was not sure what would be worse. Not knowing who you were and what was going on or knowing and not being able to change the circumstances.

Her grandma was calm tonight, not showing any signs of sundowners. She loved looking through all the old photos of her life. There was Daisy as a teen with her twin flower sister Tulip and others taken with a young handsome Henry. Lilac as a child appeared on the pages and later Kale joined the picture parade. A few snapshots of Poppy's childhood made the memory book too. The still-frame slide show was better than a motion picture for grandma.

When Daisy got dozy, Poppy tucked the covers around the frail little figure and turned off the overhead light. She still had the book bag so selected one of Xavier's returns to while-away some time before she got tired enough to drop off too.

Just when Poppy was ready to shut off her reading light, Mona returned to the room.

"Mona, we are good, don't think we need anything else for the night. Grandma is asleep. Thanks."

"I wanted to talk to you if you have a minute. I heard your grandmother's health is slipping?" Mona mentioned.

"Unfortunately, it seems to be, but there is not really a definite timetable." Poppy admitted.

"Just know I can be of assistance if you don't want to see her suffer. The end does not have to be ugly, you can take things into your own hands if you choose." Mona spoke cryptically, but Poppy was pretty sure she knew what the nurse was alluding to.

"I think I will savor every moment I have with my grandma, but thanks for your concern." Did Poppy need to sleep with one eye open? Finding a safe place to lay one's head was becoming an impossible illusion. Greener Pastures may have their own self-appointed angel of death.

It appeared Poppy was not the only person with a secret in the care center tonight.

CHAPTER 7

On any given night, there are
approximately 643,067 people experiencing
homelessness in America.

238,110 of those people are in families
25% suffer from mental illness, including
schizophrenia, bipolar disorder, and
depression
17% are considered chronically homeless
13% are fleeing domestic violence
12% are veterans

The library book bag Poppy had been toting was finally back nestled in its library home where it belonged in-spite of its roundabout overnight travels. Poppy emptied Xavier's finished books into the pile and mindlessly began sorting all the returns for shelving. She slowed to a stop at an illustrated copy of the Las Vegas Strip. The city loomed larger than life even on the glossy pages. Mammoth structures lined a brilliantly lit boulevard. Desert temperatures at that latitude must be quite warm all year she imagined. What a perfect place to live if one was homeless. A person could travel internationally without leaving one long street, moving from country to country amid a city that never sleeps.

She, she meant they, could reside in New York City at New York New York or beneath the Eiffel Tower, bathe in the waters of Venice or dwell under Luxor's sphinx pyramid. A person could even travel back in time to Excalibur or Caesar's Palace. The mega-hotels were open twenty-four hours a day with access to bathrooms and massive buffets. On restored Fremont St. was a photo of a burger joint with a large walk-on scale out front. If a person weighed over 350 pounds they ate for free. Poppy pictured herself and Xavier traveling there on a road trip. He would bring good munchies along for the drive and definitely qualify for a free heart attack burger.

If her grandmother was gone, all she would need was a bus ticket. In reality if her grandmother was gone, her finances would change enough she probably would not need to relocate to find shelter. Poppy slammed shut the cover of the book and squashed such selfish thinking. She would not go there mentally, nor likely physically either. Grandma Daisy was worth every penny. Poppy must not let her thoughts be tainted.

Thinking of her grandmother brought up another concerning thought, what was to be done about Mona?

Ethically was Poppy bound to inform Director Metcalfe about a possible grim reaper lurking among his residents, or was Mona's mission a higher calling? No, definitely not elevated. Most relatives of Greener Pasture's patients had chosen it as a safe haven for their loved ones, not as a rapid resolution or speedy exit to another realm by a Dr. Kevorkian disciple. It was still criminal to take another life, unless perhaps one were living in Oregon or some state with loose euthanasia laws.

However, Poppy could not claim for certain Mona's intent. Reading so many mysteries and thrillers could have predisposed her to make colorful assumptions. She would have to have more substantial evidence before making assertions that could potentially ruin someone's life.

Aroused from her personal revelry by Russell's arrival, Poppy realized she had been lost in her work again. If reminiscing between random pages could actually be called part of her job description. She should vow to spend as much time on her college course work as she did browsing through the returned books pile. She got distracted so easily when in a land of literature.

"Hey Poppet, how was the big guy?" Russell broke in, hoping his new nickname for her would not seem too intimate or offend in any way, but Poppy did not even seem to notice.

"I did get in his house and you are right, it was an adventure. Xavier was consuming donuts to add a fourth dimension of reality to his cop novel. I probably crossed the bounds of book courier etiquette by suggesting he do more than sit in his chair and read, possibly even pick up his pen and write a few words of his own. He must have a stored reserve of gaming knowledge to put down in ink." Poppy answered Russell's question and then some.

"I do not think you can offend the man. No worries there, he is 'insulated' you might say. He could use a swift kick in his cushy keister now and then. We have a camaraderie of sorts going back a few years, but it is difficult for me to scale his blasted steps. These wheels are not exactly all-terrain." Russell lamented good-naturedly.

"Then how did you get to know Mr. Max?" Poppy was curious.

"Well, in my earlier years you could say I was an amateur gamer. The sport works well from a chair. My online name was *RollingReader*...or R&R for short." Poppy interrupted him, "You could even be RRR or Triple R for *RollingReaderRussell*." Poppy loved alliteration.

Russell chuckled, "Yes, I suppose I could have even been Quadruple R, did you know my last name is Redmond? No one online really knew who I was anyway. Whereas, everyone knew Professor X. When I found out the Professor hailed from my hometown, we started corresponding through cyberspace occasionally. I like to take some of the credit for his new hobby and us becoming book pimps for him."

"Interesting way to put it Russell. Now perhaps you could help him find a more active interest to add to the exercising his mind…maybe throw in movement of a few limbs as well?" Poppy threw the suggestion out there.

"Unless he is into wheelchair sports. I am not much help in that category I am afraid." Russell admitted. "The responsibility might fall to you, idea girl."

"Oh, sorry Russell. I forget. You are so you, I rarely see the chair. If it isn't too forward to ask, how did you end up there, in a wheelchair?" Poppy asked anyway.

"I began here." Russell responded.

"What?" Poppy was confused.

"When I was younger, to be cool, I would tell people I was a motocross champion and it happened in a wreck during a big race competition. At times, I would change the story up and say I was in a bad car wreck that killed my family. That quieted the curious. But the truth was I was born this way."

"How? Were you injured in the womb or during the birth process?" Poppy was trying to understand. Now she was really getting personal, but it seemed like a pretty padded, accident-free environment from a lay position.

"Sort of. The lining around my spine did not close as it was supposed to. It is one of the neuro-tube defects that happen early in development. A bubble formed, and my spine grew into it outside of my body. When I was born the sack of fluid and tissue had become so large they could not fit all of my spine back into my tiny baby body, so the doctor severed my spine to close the opening. The birth defect is called spina bifida, but there are many levels of it depending which vertebra are affected. In some people you would never know. They can walk almost normally. My level was on the other end of the spectrum, but we all share one thing in common. We all have a battle wound scar at the base of our backs over the spine where it was sutured shut." Russell shared.

"Wow Russell. Sorry, I never knew. Have you always been in a wheelchair then?" Poppy continued.

"My parents let me army crawl around at home for a long time. I learned to use arm crutches for short distances from physical therapy. But for the most part, yes, I have been in a wheelchair since shortly after I was supposed to be walking. It is much easier to keep up and more convenient, usually. Can you imagine trying to carry books with crutches? The chair evens my playing field for now." Russell explained. "Who knows what the future of modern medicine will bring."

"I am sure it is frustrating at times." Poppy sympathized.

"I am pretty used to it. There are a few things I miss out on, but I would much rather have a working brain over legs, if I had to choose." Russell's outlook was impressively positive. "I feel I still have much to offer the world."

"More than much. You are amazing Russell and so independent. Thanks for sharing your story with me." Poppy was touched.

"Know I am always here for you, Poppy girl. Is there anything you want to share with me, now that you know my life story?" Russell offered.

Before she had time to deduce if this was the moment to come clean with her best work friend and closest library confidant, Jaxon Cohen strode through the library doors and headed their way.

"I will keep that in mind Russell. Thanks so much." Poppy responded as the board member's presence turned their twosome into three.

"Hello Miss Paisley, I just dropped in to see if the document search has uncovered anything?" Mr. Cohen got right to the point.

"This is Russell Redmond and he has offered to assist me in the effort." Poppy included her friend.

"Happy to lend my services to the hunt sir, but I am afraid I must currently remove myself from this trio to avoid The Tigress's pouch." said Russell as he rolled away, disappointed in his missed opportunity to get closer to the girl and possibly be her hero for the day.

"Not sure I understand. Is that library lingo or is he on a safari of some kind?" a bewildered Jaxon asked Poppy.

Poppy wondered if Jaxon Cohen was attempting a joke or truly was that oblivious. "Russell has an author's poetic way of constructing a sentence. He just has other things to do at the moment. He is more knowledgeable than I am in library matters, so he's nice to have on your team. But before I jump in 100% with both feet, I need to clear up a concern. Please know I am assigned to assist you whatever the answer."

"Okay ask away. I am curious how looking for an old document could cause concern." Jaxon puzzled. "I am not searching for secret or privileged information, only a few documents that have been misplaced over time."

"I just need to know what you plan to do with the proper documents once you uncover them. Will locating them be in the library's best interest or on behalf of J. C. Cohen Construction and Property Development investments?" Poppy asked more boldly than was her nature.

"Whoa, you are a straight shooter. You are aware that I am on the board of this library and using library property in any way for personal gain would be a conflict of interest?" Jaxon hit back. "Not that it is any of your business, but I have a project in mind that will benefit both the library and the community and not line my pockets with a penny, if that placates your concern."

Poppy's flawless fair skin blushed a faint red. "No, you are right, it is none of my business, but I do better work when I believe in the cause."

"Can you get behind and support the homeless, Miss Paisley?" Jaxon Cohen asked.

The surprise blow knocked the breath out of Poppy. Did Jaxon Cohen know her living situation? Was he toying with her? How could he, but this was an influential man with contacts and interests everywhere. She simply said, "Of course, a person would have to be heartless to not want everyone to have a home over their heads."

"Well good then, we are on the same page. My interest in the plat map or property documents have to do with a development I have in mind that would benefit both the library and those on the street. If you are interested I can share more of my vision." Jaxon Cohen offered.

"Actually, I am totally invested and passionate about both topics. Please enlighten this conclusion-jumping junior library employee and accept her full apology." Poppy humbly replied. "In fact, a few of my dearest friends happen to be living in the park as we speak, and I would be honored to play any small part in getting a roof over their heads."

Cohen continued, "I also have a vested personal interest in those less fortunate than myself who need housing. I hope to be in a position to do something about those struggling in our area at least. I was informed years ago, from a family member, that a section of land on the side of the city park near the cemetery was designated for library expansion. The idea was to place a library annex building there as an extension to their current main branch services."

"That would be wonderful." Poppy added, "But how does that affect the homeless situation? They can walk the few miles here if needed to get a book, but still won't have permanent shelter."

"My plan is more extensive and ingenuitive. I need the documents to also determine if I can combine the library with temporary housing. My inspiration is to build a library with bunks or a homeless hotel with a reading room for those who need a place to go for a night or more. It will not be permanent housing, but a way-station. Especially in adverse weather conditions, it will prevent the unfortunate from far more unfortunate circumstances and hopefully help them turn things around." Jaxon got excited and flushed when sharing his dream, which only enhanced his chiseled features.

Poppy was more than 100% in and sorry she had misjudged the man, "Mr. Cohen I would be honored to be your library-looking-leg of this great venture and your go-to-girl in anything else you might need to accomplish your goal."

In answer, C. Jaxon Cohen extended his manicured hand and they shook on it like actual partners. Poppy giggled like a school girl. What had she committed to? In reality she was the one with a conflict of interest and personal gain to be acquired from this project.

CHAPTER 8

Homelessness affects men more than women.
At least 70% to 85% of all homeless are men.
A 59-year-old homeless man in North Carolina
once held up a bank for $1 in order to be
sent to jail and receive the healthcare he
needed. Homeless life is indeed hard, but
not of all of it has to be dreary. Making
the best of a bad situation, there has been
a National Hobo Convention in Britt, Iowa
every year for the past century. They even
crown a King and Queen. Based on the
percentages, there are a lot more candidates
available to be crowned king, than queen.

The week wobbled by in Poppy's routine, yet non-routine world...regular visits to see Grandma Daisy and spy on Mona, stops by the park to check in on Chet, Bernie and Obi-Wan, working at the library and staying afterward to study for school, intermingled with basic life maintaining ventures filled her days. Today she was scheduled to present story time for their preschool crowd, one of her favorite library duties, if not her absolute favorite.

The elegantly illustrated *Miss Maple's Seeds* by Eliza Wheeler was charming her young audience. Poppy adored the book too. It was one of her best-loved in the juvenile section. Miss Maple was looking for orphan seeds that did not get planted to take them home until spring. This compassionately minded fairytale mouse was tending to the homeless in her own little world Poppy mused. "Take care my little ones for the world is big and you are small." Poppy read to the engrossed children. While in the story Miss Maple read "flower tales" by firefly light to those in her imaginary realm. It was a deliciously delightful story to consume. "Don't be afraid, raindrops help us grow." she continued reading. Then with the last spring petals drifting down from the sky…the misplaced seeds were off to find roots of their own in various places.

Nearly all flowers and trees started from seeds and put down roots to grow. What was her Poppy flower seed? And where was she to put down her roots to grow? Perhaps she needed a Miss Maple in her life. The children's expectant faces looked up at her and Poppy realized she had finished the book and they were patiently waiting for the next selection lying on her lap. *The Lady in the Box* by Ann McGovern rested there.

In McGovern's story it is wintertime in the city and freezing cold, but not everyone is inside and warm. Ben and his sister Lizzie know that there is a kind-looking lady who lives outside in a box over a warm air vent and they want to help her.

Okay, maybe Poppy had loosely centered today's reading list on a common theme, that may or may not overlap with her real life, slightly. The book before her was quite tender and definitely a worthwhile read. Ben, who appears to be around eight, describes how he and his sister bring food and a scarf to a homeless woman, Dorrie, who lives in a box over a heat vent near a deli in their neighborhood. In doing so, they thereby bend their mother's rules about talking to strangers--or at least interpret them widely.

There were more printed words on a page than was probably age appropriate to hold these munchkins' interest. The book was more fodder for her own thoughts anyway. She tucked it to the bottom of the pile and selected the next one to read. The thirty minutes passed pleasantly, interspersed with random questions from the youthful crowd that at times made Poppy laugh. Time sped by far too fast in the circle of carpet squares and story time was over. She longed to give each child a hug as they left, but Ms. Moriah Bengal had strictly forbidden her from the gesture. There was always liability when touching children. So, she sent them off with a warm smile and wave instead.

Time to get back to searching for the missing library property document, which supposedly existed. She and Russell spent at least an hour every shift systematically going through each possible section where it may have been shelved, who knew how long ago. They had yet to succeed on their mission.

Russell was scheduled today to trade out their American Indian display for another with a few relics from the Byzantine Empire. The new pieces dated pre-1400 A.D. from what was now Constantinople in Turkey. The library had two glass display cases where items they took in on loan were displayed for a few months at a time. Russell was responsible to catalogue what they received and also package the items to be returned. Trading obsidian arrowheads for ancient gold jewelry seemed like a step up to Poppy. Everyone had their own idea of what treasure was she supposed. Russell's current task meant she was on her own today in the pre-computer docx search.

Not long after the little ones dispersed, she heard Russell's hushed voice calling her name in a hissing whisper. Poppy tiptoe sprinted to the glass display cases as quickly and quietly as she was able, hoping Russell was not injured in any way. But when she crossed the twenty plus feet to her destination, there before her eyes was an image that was more likely found in one of her novels than in real life. At the base of the old wooden display, where the case met its legs, was a slot that opened, and a drawer had partially slid forward to expose a hidden chamber.

"I couldn't open it all the way without you here to share the moment." Russell said.

"Wowzers Russell! How in the world did you find the drawer, it must have been there for over a hundred years?" Poppy marveled.

"Well, I guess my point of view from chair level is good for something. I was sitting here, trying to get close enough to take out the Indian artifacts. As I slid my wheelchair as close as I could to the display, one of the armrests slid under the structure and must have triggered some mechanism because this sliver of an opening appeared immediately." Russell caught her up on the exploit.

"Just like in a National Treasure movie. You are our own Nicholas Cage, or Ben Gates I guess." Poppy jested.

"Shall we see what is inside, assistant Abigail?" Russell followed Poppy's movie reference cue.

The two librarian adventurers slowly slid open the long undisclosed drawer wondering what would be revealed. Would there be more display items left from days gone by? Nope, a thin stack of paperwork, yellowed with age, nested between the dusty planks.

"This could be our eureka." Russell admitted. "I should probably call over Moriah, but let's see if we can figure out what we have here first."

Russell gently lifted from the secret drawer a short stack of yellowed papers. The top page was written in old-school script and definitely had something to do with the St. Anthony Library. The first sheet did not look fragile enough to crumble, so he lifted and turned over it over to view the next. The second page appeared to be some kind of legal property deed. There was a genuine possibility that these papers could be the ones Cohen was looking for.

Poppy felt like doing a happy dance but was not sure what that would look like to Russell. "It does look like some kind of old documents, I guess I should give Mr. Cohen a call to come check out our discovery and see if there is anything he can use." Poppy suggested. "Thank you for sharing the moment with me Russell. It was magically memorable."

"Can we please savor our discovery as a duo for a while longer before you call in the cavalry?" Russell pled gently.

The two gazed at their find for a few moments before gently removing the sheets from the drawer, careful not to damage the fragile pages. "Thanks for giving us a moment before having to share." Russell sighed. Poppy went to make the call and Russell to inform The Tigress.

It did not take long for Jaxon Cohen to arrive. He looked calm and collected on the exterior as he sauntered through the doors, but Poppy could feel his suppressed energy buzzing just under the surface. Jaxon was full of anticipation with his jawline tensely clenched. Without a word, she led him towards the back of the building. They passed by Misty manning the front desk. Poppy glanced over and saw that the butterfly aficionado was wearing dangling winged earrings to accent a large Monarch appliquéd on the back of her jean jacket. All the ensemble needed was some bedazzling. Jaxon Cohen did not seem to notice any distractions. He was single-minded on this brief quest, only interrupting his focus to ask Poppy where the papers had been discovered.

Moriah had taken the uncovered treasure into a back room where all sensitive materials were handled. The pages were splayed out side by side across a counter surface. This allowed them to be read with limited handling to preserve the integrity of the paper. Jaxon Cohen methodically perused the pages before him. "Could I take a couple of them with me for my lawyer to look over? It looks like there may be something I can use here. Dad said they had been tucked away for safe keeping. That was an understatement."

Moriah shuddered in horror, "These original documents will not be allowed to leave the library premises. You can bring the barrister here or take some non-flash photos for him to look over if you prefer."

"I will snap a few shots with my phone, but if not legible enough for him, I guess I can bring my legal man by. Thank you for locating these. I am quite grateful." Mr. Cohen expressed as he glanced over at Poppy.

Poppy and Russell left to let the other two conclude their business. It was an anticlimactic ending to their grand exploit. But before Jaxon Cohen exited the library, he paused at the desk and directly addressed Poppy who had joined Misty up front.

"I would like to reward you for your efforts Miss Paisley. The Library Board of Directors is having a function where I plan to present my ideas to the group. It is mostly a social event. Would you be willing to go as my plus one? I feel it would be appropriate, not only because you discovered the papers that may allow the building to happen, but also since your feelings about the homeless mirror my own. The dinner is next Friday night and I believe the dress is black tie, if you would like to attend."

Poppy did not know where to begin. First of all, she was not even the one who found the important papers, Russell was, but Mr. Cohen had not mentioned that 'plus two' was a possibility. She did have a vested interest in the homeless and a catered event full of delectable taste treats, or any non-institution or fast food, sounded mouthwatering. Not to mention the fact Jaxon Cohen was an attractive man and she had not had a date in over a year. She never knew where to be picked up, so had avoided them. The explanation that filtered out of Poppy's mouth was merely, "Oh, that sounds wonderful, but I am afraid I don't have a dress for that swanky of an event." She hoped he did not think she was fishing to get him to provide one.

As disappointed Jaxon started to respond, the usually timid Butterfly Queen chose this exact moment to decide to open up. "Actually, I have a gown that may be suitable. I know I am a few inches shorter than you are Poppy, but I think we are close enough in size to make it work. You are welcome to come by and try it on if interested."

Poppy was more interested in going to Misty's home in hopes of catching a glimpse of butterfly world than she was in wearing the dress. Who knew what kind of frock Misty would deem suitable for a high brow social affair. Surely there would be at least one butterfly on it. But the old saying "beggars could not be choosers" was definitely true in this case.

Jaxon Cohen while waiting for Poppy's reply, gallantly offered. "I am sure you would look lovely in whatever fashion you choose to wear. The women come to these affairs in all extremes. What do you think? Would you be willing to accompany me?"

Poppy wanted to say yes, but the many reasons she should say no, kept playing bumper cars in her brain. Finally, just before it felt extremely awkward, Poppy replied. "Mr. Cohen, I will give you a tentative yes, but need to find a dress. Misty, I will take you up on the generous offer, if you are truly serious, and come by to check out the garment."

"It is a plan then, unless I hear differently. Where should I pick you up, say at around seven o'clock on Friday? Jaxon asked.

This was the part Poppy was dreading. There was no way on earth she was going to ask C. Jaxon Cohen to pick her up at her car parked in the cemetery, the YMCA or near a city park bench. That left Greener Pastures or the library. Both places had pros and cons. If she said at Green Pastures, she could use the excuse her grandmother would love to see her all dressed up. Or, he already knew how to get to the library and that would not let him creep deeper into her life.

"How about just here at the library, again unless you hear differently." Poppy suggested. She knew it was strange, but the best she could come up with.

"If that is what you prefer. I like a woman with mystery." Jaxon chuckled. "Until next Friday." Then he was gone.

Poppy could not believe what she had just done. What had she gotten herself into? She may still be able to escape graciously if needed. She was definitely not date material for St. Anthony Library's best-looking board member, even if he was single and available.

Misty woke Poppy from her mental reel of an awkward episode of The Bachelor, where she definitely would not be the girl to get the rose. "You can drop by tomorrow after work or pretty much whenever works for you, as long as you give me some notice," Misty offered.

"If you are sure. Yes, I would love to try on your dressy outfit and maybe see your butterfly collection too, if that is okay and not too much to ask. Let's plan on tomorrow?" Poppy did not think she could handle any more excitement today.

It had been a day for surprises...she and Russell, mostly Russell, found some lost wonders, *The* Jaxon Cohen, board member, sort of asked her out, and she had been given a coveted pass to enter butterfly world. What more could any girl want, homeless or otherwise. Now she just had to hope she could say, "yes to the dress" and not embarrass herself with her less-than ideal living or pick-up logistics. Then there was just one other tiny thing that haunted her. The lingering guilt seeping into her soul was going to be difficult to shake... for leaving Russell out of the elegant affair that he deserved to attend too.

CHAPTER 9

830,120 year-round beds are available in the range of housing projects. About half of those beds are dedicated to people currently experiencing homelessness. This includes: 1) Emergency Shelters that provide temporary or nightly shelter beds to people experiencing homelessness. 2) Transitional Housing that provides homeless people up to 24 months of housing and supportive services. 3) Safe Havens that provide temporary shelter and services to hard-to-serve individuals. According to the US Department of Housing and Urban Development (HUD) most people are spending the night either in homeless shelters or in some sort of short-term transitional housing. Slightly more than a third are living in cars or under bridges or are in some other way living unsheltered.

Poppy took the bus back towards her old neighborhood and got off at the Tooterville stop. Misty had given Poppy the address of her home and they were to meet there around six-o'clock. The area was not far from her grandmother's former apartment so felt familiar, but Poppy had never been on this street. She walked past a couple of low-end apartment buildings and a few forlorn fourplexes to find the diminutive domicile tucked back off the road at the back of a vacant lot. She was surprised to find a free-standing home in this neighborhood. It must have been a servant's quarters back in the day, built behind a larger home that was now gone.

Poppy could have identified the home, even without the house number, from the butterfly mailbox. The metal tube was painted in vibrant colors and had plastic wings attached. The small home it serviced was more a rundown cottage, verging on a shack, but appeared tidy behind the peeling paint and chipped cement stoop. There were flowers planted in patches of dirt on each side of the front door. Her mother would have liked that. Poppy wondered if they were located there to lure butterflies.

The curtains over the larger window on the front side of the house parted a few inches and shortly after, Misty opened the weather-beaten door. If Xavier's house took her to another world, Misty's went to another solar system. The mode of decor centered entirely around the delicate winged species Misty loved. There were butterfly throw pillows, butterfly paintings and photographs, even a wing-backed chair had been constructed to cradle a person in the wings of a butterfly. It was the ultimate butterfly indoctrination. Poppy's head spun 360 degrees around the room to try to absorb it all. The only non-winged photo was of a very young girl with curly hair, in a butterfly dress of course. "This is truly amazing, I have always wanted to see your butterfly room, Misty."

"Oh, this is only my living room, the butterfly room is through that door." Misty pointed towards a small door to her right. "Please enter as quickly as you can when I open it, to prevent them from flying out."

The real butterfly room was warm and humid. Live butterflies flew over and around their heads in copious numbers. Hundreds more were impaled and framed behind glass on the walls. Misty could see Poppy taking in wall after wall of her departed pets, "I cannot bear to get rid of so much beauty when they die, so I preserve them for all time in this sanctuary. The north wall is covered with those from the Pieridae family and the south wall those from the Parnassas Clodius group. They are a high-altitude genus of the swallow tail family. On the west and east walls, I have organized them more by color and wing patterns. Each is so unique. And there is still some space for my collection to grow."

Poppy was mesmerized. It was unreal, yet totally real, more unique than she could have imagined in her wildest dreams. She felt like she was in the winged insect version of Jurassic Park. The beauty was intoxicating and the energy in the room invigorating. She struggled to put her feelings into words. "Misty this is beyond beyond. You should open this to the public, not your home, but find a place to share what you have created."

"I should never have shown you. This is not for the public. It is very private. I just chose to share it with you." said Misty protectively.

"I apologize Misty. It is just so cool, and I have never seen anything like it and know others would find it fascinating as well, but I understand. (Even though she was not sure she did). Not everything has to be for everyone and I can tell this space is precious to you." Poppy retracted her earlier words and watched Misty physically calm down and be more at ease again. "Where did you find all of these butterflies?"

"I captured some in various locations, but mostly ordered them online. Let's go back into the other room and I will get the dress for you." Misty said.

"First, please let me take in everything I can, this may be the only time I get to see something so spectacularly otherworldly." Poppy requested, as a yellow and brown butterfly landed briefly on her nose before fluttering on. She sat down on the floor and let the loveliest members of the insect family swirl around her and brush gently with their feather soft wigs. Poppy was transfixed. "Anything else I should see? What is behind those double doors on the west wall?"

A look like terror crossed Misty's countenance before she ushered Poppy rapidly out of the room. Poppy had pushed some unknown button that caused immediate ejection but was still thoroughly enthralled by the experience she had been given. The room was a mixture of magical creatures with an element of disturbing. "Thank you, Misty, I will never forget that. I am so glad I came even if the dress doesn't work."

"The dress is in the image of the Lycaena, copper colored with black spots and gossamer-wings. I absolutely had to have it. My mother purchased it for me for a prom that I ended up not being able to attend. I have never had the heart to get rid of it." Misty explained as she presented the garment to Poppy.

Poppy was not sure if it was the most gorgeous clothing creation she had ever seen or a monstrosity. The fabric was airy, gauze-like and layered, an extra piece flowing back from each side truly like gossamer wings. The coppery color would either clash with or accent her auburn locks and the black markings added interest. If it fit, did she dare wear it? Could anyone pull off such an audacious fashion. Jaxon said women wore about anything, but he had never seen this dress. Misty watched for Poppy's reaction from her bi-spectacled eyes.

"That is a very impressive gown, are you sure you are comfortable to share?" Poppy asked. "If so, is there a room to try it on?"

Misty led Poppy to the small bathroom down an extremely short hallway and waited expectantly at the door. "I want to see it when you get it on."

Poppy pulled the filmy fabric over her head. It felt like it fit, but with all the layers, a perfect fit did not matter much. The mirror was not large enough to see below her shoulders, so she emerged from the powder room to get her review. A gasp arose from Misty, so Poppy assumed it must look either breathtaking or utterly terrifying.

"I always knew it would be wonderful." Misty sighed. Poppy looked down, maybe this place had affected her perspective, but the dress did look eerily elegant from this vantage point. Now she wondered if she would have the nerve to wear it.

"I feel like I get to go to the ball vicariously if you wear my dress there." Misty said wistfully. "Do one twirl for me and if you put the elastic bands over your wrist the fabric pieces look like wings. Don't you just love it?"

"It is beyond anything I could have dreamed of Misty. Truly. Thank you. I am grateful." Poppy was breaking out of her chrysalis and going to the board dinner as a butterfly. This would be interesting.

She changed out of the dress and turned to leave but noticed the framed little butterfly girl again and asked Misty if it was a photo of her as a child. "No, that is Aporia, named after a butterfly whose white wings have black veins running through them." She answered.

"Who is Aporia? Is she a relative?" Poppy asked.

"Aporia is my daughter." Misty admitted.

"You have a daughter? I had no idea. Where is she now?" Poppy pried.

A distant look came over Misty's eyes, "Aporia is away for a while preparing for her future."

Poppy could tell the topic was closed and wanted to avoid another butterfly room incident, where she had pressed too far. Perhaps Aporia was at a boarding school, but not likely on their salaries. Maybe she had an absent rich father who was providing some special schooling or training for her? Misty really was a mystery. At least she had gotten to experience the butterfly room and was leaving with a butterfly costume to boot.

"I promise to take special care of your dress and return it dry cleaned right after next Friday, Misty. You are very generous. Thanks again." Poppy was not sure if her company was wanted further or if Misty was ready to have her leave. The woman was impossible to read. Poppy did not plan to weasel an overnight stay but sleeping with the butterflies would be really something. Her small workmate stood still without offering anything further, so Poppy took her exit. She left bearing a lightweight bundle of fabric delight.

The trunk of her car did not seem like an appropriate place to store the borrowed fashion creation, so Poppy decided to take the dress to Greener Pastures to keep in G-ma Daisy's closet until Friday. She wished she had remembered to ask Misty about Xavier, perhaps they could form an eccentric friendship. The two recluses with such extreme decorating styles could be balanced company for one another. Or on the other end, may have absolutely nothing in common and make each other feel more-lonely.

It was nearly dark when Poppy arrived at the care center. Hopefully it would work well to stay here for the night. The smells and sounds of Greener Pastures all blended to make what one could only describe as a non-homey cocktail as she walked down the corridors to her grandmother's room. From a distance, she observed Mona ducking into Miss Whitley's room up ahead. Still toting the frock, Poppy paused outside Delta Dawn's door to eavesdrop. No surprise to hear Mona discussing Gerald with her patient, it was the constant concern and topic of conversation in room #223. But Poppy's blood went cold when she heard Mona ask Miss Whitley if she would like to go meet Gerald tonight. Mona was getting ready to fulfill a line from the song…*meet him in his mansion in the sky.*

Poppy tucked the mounds of fabric under her arm and redirected her steps to Director Metcalfe's office, praying he would not have left for the night. The two nearly collided as she turned the corner to his office. "Miss Paisley, I was just heading home, it has been a crazy day here…"

"I need to talk to you." Poppy interjected.

"Could it perhaps wait until tomorrow, your grandmother seems to be holding stable for now and I am bone tired. I won't be much good to anyone." Metcalfe replied.

"No actually it is a matter of life and death and cannot wait until morning or one of your patients may not have a morning." Poppy sounded a bit dramatic, but it was the truth.

"All right. What is the emergency?" The director asked without even taking her back into his office. "Many of our residents' lives are at the corner of life and death once they arrive between our walls."

Poppy poured out her unverified suspicions, including what she had just heard.

Mr. Metcalfe did not seem as shocked as she suspected he might be. "That is a tall accusation, let me talk with Miss Mona before calling in the authorities. Perhaps there is some other rational explanation for the words you heard."

"But it has to be now, there is not time to watch and wait. Who knows how many others have met a similar fate here." Poppy felt panicked. Were elderly lives disposable?

"I will send Mona home for the night before I leave and request a meeting with her first thing in the morning, after I have slept on it and my head is clear. I promise. Do not think I condone this sort of practice. Your grandmother and the others will not be in danger tonight." His shoulders sagged as he headed to Miss Whitley's room to make sure Delta Dawn did not complete her chorus this evening.

Poppy plopped into the recliner in G-ma Daisy's room, buried in the layers of copper with black dots. Maybe she would just sleep here all night with the dress as her blanket and not move an inch. She was not sure she could endure another minute of strangeness or abnormal behavior. But really, what would be considered normal in her circle? She was a twenty-three-year-old sitting in a dementia center underneath a butterfly costume. She could not imagine what her life might look like at seventy-three if she lived to arrive there.

Grandma stirred and looked up at Poppy. Her wrinkled skin tone was a waxy yellow under the overhead light. It appeared her body was failing along with her mind. Poppy did not speak. It was better to pretend all was well and things would be different soon.

"Poppy is that you dear girl? What do you have with you, or all over you?" She asked like she had never forgotten.

Poppy was afraid to answer and break the spell but did not want to be rude. "A dress for a fancy function grandma."

"How fun. Would you try in on for me sweetie? I would love to see my beautiful girl in her finest."

When Poppy emerged from the bathroom cocoon as a butterfly, her grandmother had fallen asleep. Poppy did not dare wake her. She would rather hold on to the moment of tender mercy when she was remembered. Pulling the chair closer to the institutional bed, she slid down the side rail and lay her head with one cheek on her grandma's bony chest. An aged, gnarled hand lifted from the covers and stroked the reddish waves of hair in an autonomic act.

Thus, Poppy ended her unusual day dressed as a butterfly, resting in Greener Pastures, with her wings draped across the woman she loved dearly.

CHAPTER 10

Fifty percent of the homeless population is over the age of 50. These individuals often face additional health and safety risks associated with age. They are more prone to injuries from falls, and may suffer from cognitive impairment, vision or hearing loss, major depression, and chronic conditions like diabetes and arthritis.

Friday night Poppy dreaded waiting at the library for her date. She had dressed at the care center, so G-ma Daisy got to see the gown, but unfortunately grandma no longer knew who Poppy was, so was startled by the butterfly woman in her room.

Director Metcalfe had taken Poppy aside and shared the results of his confrontation with Mona. He placed Mona on probation and she would be monitored more closely. He hesitated to fire her, for if indeed there was a problem, he feared she would continue her self-assigned mission at another facility. It was not difficult to get a CNA position at a nursing home and for now he had no proof to accompany the accusations. He would rather know where she was and what she was up to at this point. His decision was not comforting to Poppy, but he was the one in charge. She did ask that Mona not be assigned to room #217.

Misty helped Poppy perform a few final touches to her make-up and hair in the library restroom. She added a pair of her best butterfly earrings, then swept back one side of Poppy's auburn hair with a mother of pearl butterfly comb. The overall effect was full on butterfly queen, but Poppy did not complain. Misty's assistance was sweet, even if slightly strange.

Poppy hid in the girl's lavatory as long as she could, hoping Russell would go home and she would not have to face him. But when she emerged, he still was there waiting for her.

"I had to see you before I headed home and am extremely glad I waited." Russell smiled. "You're always a one of a kind flower-girl."

"I guess that is a good thing? I need to apologize to you Russell. I am so sorry." Poppy said.

"What for? Breaking my heart?" Russell joked, but in his mind added…. "for letting a man less worthy take you out on a date, when I am dying to go out with you?"

"Funny Russell. No, this should have been you not me." Poppy admitted.

"Sorry, not sure the dress would fit me, and you make a much better butterfly." He found it best to make light and laugh through the difficulty's life dealt him.

"Not the dress you goof, but you should have had the opportunity to go to this event, not me. You are the one who found the document that is going to help Jaxon Cohen complete his project." Poppy said dejectedly. "I have felt awful since I told him I would go and did not insist he invite you."

"No worries. I am positive finding the plat deed was not the main reason you were the one he asked. I wouldn't want to go with him anyway. Now, if I were going out with you, that would be another story. Go enjoy yourself. I am fine about this. Honestly." Russell told her. Poppy was pretty sure Russell was the kind of man who would say those things even if he felt badly about what had happened. He was unfailingly gracious and positive, but she did feel better.

"I know I have said it before, but for real, I am not sure what I would do without you Russell. You are too good to me. I will try to save a dessert somewhere amid these folds of fabric for you to try." Poppy offered.

"Not unless you want Misty to have your head. Do you see how she looks at you in that dress? It is almost in reverence. I fear for you if you should damage the flowing butterfly in any way. I'm good." And Russell seemed like he was.

Misty let Poppy know that Jaxon Cohen had pulled up out front. To prevent the library staff from feeling like parents who were sending their little girl out on her first date, she headed out the door on her own and met the library board member mid-stairway. He almost rushed right past, before realizing who was encased in the orange wave floating towards him. Poppy had not put the elastic over her wrists to form the wings, but the impact was still enough to stop Mr. Cohen in his tracks.

Poppy halted and embarrassedly sputtered. "You don't have to take me. I know this is a bit over-the-top, but the best I could do."

"No, you misunderstand. You take my breath away. I think you are lovely. You can be my visual aid for the night. We are trying to help the homeless become the butterflies they each are, underneath their many layers of clothing cocoons." Jaxon improvised.

"Should I put something on over this until you present then?" Poppy asked.

"And hide all that, never. You will just peak their interest for what is coming. And we better get going." Mr.

Cohen took Poppy's arm to complete their joint journey to the bottom of the stairs and opened the door of his black BMW for her to hop in. Well, there was not much hopping when you were wearing yards and yards of flowing chiffon, Poppy gathered her skirt and stuffed herself into the leather seat.

The ride there was pleasant. Soft music was playing on the radio, so the two didn't have to talk much. When they arrived at the conference center, suddenly extremely nervous, Poppy had to force herself out of the car and into the building. Her feet became leaden blocks, each weighing a thousand pounds and sweat trickled down the small of her back. Questioning eyes watched as the butterfly entered the room. Poppy felt like a gawky Cinderella whose fairy godmother had gotten the spell wrong.

Jaxon Cohen navigated the room like a professional race car driver, introducing her as he wove between conversations of stylishly dressed couples and stopping to speak with only a limited number of those present. Tables circled the edges of the space filled with a variety of appetizers. Waiters carried even more food on trays, offering their tasty wares to guests as they walked by.

Poppy wanted to try one of everything but grabbed a stuffed mushroom and asparagus spear wrapped with bacon and cheese as they cruised by. The caterer appeared to be encouraging vegetables, enticing the crowd by wrapping them in meat and dairy. The results were delicious.

A gaggle of sophisticated women near her age were eyeing Poppy up and down as she stood next to Jaxon. Above his business conversation, Poppy could hear their hushed comments, most likely snarky, being exchanged in the all-female circle. One of socialites turned to Poppy and inquired about the designer of her dress, followed by a ripple of submerged laughter through her backup gal-pals.

Poppy was not going to let them ruin her big night out. Her life circumstances did not lend well to being thin-skinned, so she calmly coughed up a clever answer. "I am wearing a Lycaena by Misty." She offered as she removed herself from the junior high-ish mean girls.

An elegant elderly woman, younger than her grandmother, but older than Lilac would have been, gently grabbed Poppy by the elbow and glided her to a safer space. "Don't let those primping dandies bother you, they are just jealous you are brave enough to pull off such a stunning creation, when they must remain fashion clones."

Poppy liked her rescuer immediately. "I know it is not the latest style, but I was just grateful to have something formal to wear to this event."

"Phewy, some fashions are timeless and classic, and your gown is definitely in that category. I have not seen you at one of these stuffy library events before, what brings you here with our handsome and eligible Jaxon Cohen?" The unknown woman's kindness had entitled her to further probing in Poppy's estimation.

"I work at the library and am assisting Mr. Cohen with a new project he is presenting." Poppy perhaps exaggerated her worth but wanted to sound like she belonged.

"Well, it is delightful to have new blood at this inbred gathering. I am Mrs. Wentworth, Camellia, should you need an escape route at any time." Mrs. Wentworth smiled.

Of course, the name of this woman made total sense. The buds and leaves of flowering Camellia plants made a tea that offered comfort and healing. She was a human manifestation of the flower's name. No wonder Poppy felt a kinship. "And I was named for another flower, the Poppy."

Jaxon joined their little posy bouquet. "Sounds like introductions have already been made. Thank you for entertaining my guest when I was negligent Mrs. Wentworth."

"My pleasure young man. I hope our paths cross again this evening or very soon. Your young lady brings a breath of fresh air to the premises." Camellia responded before she strode on to save others in need of her services.

"Do you know who that woman is?" Jaxon asked incredulously.

"Mrs. Camellia Wentworth." Poppy answered.

"Yes, but did you know she and her husband are the largest donors on the foundation board?" Jaxon asked. "Tonight, is not only for the library board members, but also for the foundation and any other large independent donors. You did good work befriending her."

"Actually, she took me under her wing, forgive the metaphor in light of what I am wearing." Poppy coyly smiled.

"However, it happened, it was fortuitous. Now are you ready for our show?" Jason asked.

"What? Am I doing something I was not aware of?" Poppy queried.

"Just lend a shoulder of support and share your passion if called upon." Jaxon teased. "Let's go."

As the power point progressed, Poppy had to admit she was impressed. The man knew his business and how to present a project. If she had any resources, she would be inspired to empty her shallow pockets to help him fund his dream. Jaxon Cohen began with the history of the St. Anthony Library, its chartered vision and the services it provided for the community. There was a slide, somewhere in the middle, of the documents she and Russell had located and near the end, a mockup drawing of the project he had in mind.

The sketch showed a building, part library annex and part homeless hotel. The building was situated on the parcel of land where the park met the cemetery property, Poppy's neck of the woods. The structure included a small library on one side, with a residence or hotel for those that needed temporary housing on the opposite side, bound in the middle by a computer area and foyer connecting the two. The space could be shared equally, or the focus could lean more heavily on the library function with a bunk house added, or the housing shelter could be the main event with a reading nook on the side. Jaxon said there was still time for input from the group. The needs of the community and ideas of people present would be considered.

Poppy watched, proud to play any part in such an exciting plan. Then a slide flashed on the screen that caught her breath. Chet, her Chet from the park, was larger than life and in living color. Was he the poster child for the project? She wondered how that happened. Then she noticed the named below his photo...Chester J. Cohen. He was Jaxon's father? Chet had mentioned more than once he had a son that he wanted Poppy to meet, but she never could have guessed the connection between the two men. No wonder Jaxon was interested in the homeless, but was he too ashamed to mention that his father was also in that category? She shut off her thoughts long enough to hear Jaxon say, "I want to dedicate the building to my father Chester Cohen. He started the construction and development business I run today. Our company will provide all the labor and building materials at our cost in his name and honor."

This Mr. Cohen left out one important part. His father, the other Mr. Cohen, was currently a resident of the very same area where he hoped to build the structure. How could Jaxon let his own father live on the streets? Chet was sharp. He did not come across mentally ill at all, maybe Bernie could be, but this made no sense to her. Poppy decided not to let Jaxon know, just yet, that she knew his father and his living situation. There had to be more to the story. Applause filled the room. Jaxon had finished and opened up a Q & A session. Poppy only caught half of what was being said. She had her own questions that needed answering, but not now.

Then another horrifying realization hit her. Poppy had not thought through the ride home situation. She had been so focused on the pickup plan and what to wear, that a drop-off plan had not been formed. Maybe she could be gawky Cinderella again and run out at the stroke of midnight leaving a shoe, nothing like a glass slipper, on her exit. But really, what was she going to do? It was long before midnight and she was not a fairytale character. What were her non-storybook options? Think girl, think.

She could not ask Jaxon to drop her off at the library where he had acquired her, it was now closed. The care center was probably locked down as well. It was like a fortress at night due to dementia patients' Houdini-like abilities to escape. Definitely she could not be returned to the cemetery, or the city park, or her car. All locations would shoot off major red flags as bright as flares.

At Misty's she could use the excuse she needed to return the dress, but that left her in a rough neighborhood if Misty was not home or if she could not rouse her. And

Misty did not have much extra room to house guests. Poppy was not ready for the easiest solution, to tell Jaxon the truth.

She knew Russell would readily welcome her if she chose to go there, but she was not ready to share her lack of living quarters with him yet either. Not only did she have too much pride, it was easier and less embarrassing to share problems with total strangers.

That was it. Total stranger... Xavier's place. Xavier Max had a ton of unaccounted for rooms she could stow away in. And if she could not get in, the Max home was close to a bus stop that was in a safe neighborhood. Current crisis averted. Now she just needed to endure the rest of this evening without exposing to C. Jaxon Cohen that she knew his dirty little secret, and not let him know hers.

CHAPTER 11

One quarter of homeless people are children. HUD reports that on any given night, over 138,000 of the homeless in the U.S. are children under the age of 18, and thousands of these children are unaccompanied by adults. Another federal program, No Child Left Behind, defines 'homeless children' more broadly and includes those who are sharing the housing of other persons due to economic hardship; living in cars, parks, bus or train stations; or awaiting foster-care placement. Under this definition, the National Center for Homeless Education reported in September 2014 that local school districts reported over 1 million homeless children in public schools. Fatherless homes produce 90% of the homeless children as well as 70% of high school dropouts, and 85% of kids in detention facilities.

Xavier Max was unusually unruffled by a butterfly woman's pre-midnight arrival at his doorstep. He definitely had become desensitized by his alternate cyber-world, if this seemed semi-normal to him. Poppy spied his reading lamp shining from the pastel covered window when she and Jaxon pulled up at the driveway gates. With hope of entrance, she mumbled something about "Uncle Max", thanked Jaxon for the outing and hustled from his car. Jaxon waited for the door to open before driving away baffled.

Xavier merely said, "I see you don't have my new books with you." Then he asked two questions. "Should I suppose you are a moth, arriving at this time of night attracted to my porch light?" And, "are you alright?" After deciphering she was not in any danger, nor had she been harmed in any way, Xavier offered her the guest room for the night.

"All I need is one of your old t-shirts, if I could bother you for one, and an empty couch and I will be out of here first bus in the morning." Poppy requested. She was grateful that Xavier Max was an ultimate gentleman and host. He did not press her for details, even though certainly curious, and Poppy was too mortified to freely volunteer the information. The World of Warcraft t-shirt was tent-like comfy and the couch in the gaming den more than adequate, but Poppy's night was restless. She was out the front door when the first light of morning painted streaks across the dark sky.

The early bus riders were as oblivious as her nighttime host had been, or just too sleep deprived to notice a rumpled human butterfly seated on a plastic bench in their midst. Poppy was able to get to her car, retrieve fresh clothing and drop the dress off at the cleaners all by eight o'clock A.M. She didn't need to go in until the closing shift at work and needed to run a few errands beforehand.

Her first goal was to find Chet. He and Bernie were already seated on their favorite bench with Obi-Wan lying across Chet's scuffed wing-tip shoes when Poppy happened upon them. Obi-Wan Kenobi was such a docile dog. She pondered briefly where the trio stowed their belongings. There was no old shopping cart to push, they didn't have a large cardboard box for shelter and she was pretty sure they did not have a car buried in the brush. Poppy determined they must be wearing their minimal possessions on their backs or stuffed in the backpack tucked beneath them.

"Glorious morning Miss Magnolia! So glad you brought us some sunshine." Chet called out when he saw her. Bernie shielded her eyes from the actual sun and gave Poppy a missing-tooth smile.

Poppy was not sure where to begin breaching the awkward subject of patriarch-ship. "How are you three fairing today. I was hoping to find you here and doing well."

"All's good and well when you have so few possessions to worry about, cute Buttercup. We are more interested to hear about Grandma and yourself." Chet replied.

"G-ma Daisy is sliding down the slippery slope of declining health, but she remembered me for a sliver of time this week, which was pretty wonderful. Then I had a huge opportunity getting to go to a library board function last night." Poppy jumped in. "In fact, I think I saw your photo there Chet and may have met your son."

Chet seemed pleased, but not shocked. "Now that is fun news. You finally met my Jaxon? He is a good man."

Poppy was flabbergasted. "Chet, a good man does not usually leave his father to live in a park."

"Jaxon has done the best he could under the circumstances. The boy revived the business I devastated and is trying to put things right. My situation is my own fault." Chet replied.

"We all make mistakes, but some are bigger than others. It is one thing to have a business fail, another to not step up and take care of your own family." Poppy took comfort thinking of Daisy lying in a clean bed surrounded by warm walls. "This project he is doing is just balm for his guilty conscious."

"Possibly. But he needs to feel no guilt. I was an adult who made poor choices. I did not turn to my family when I should have and ended up here. Don't blame Jaxon. Be there for him, however you can. He has his own demons to deal with." Chet reasoned.

"I am not sure there is anything I can do, even if I wanted to. He probably thinks I am a freak anyway. I went to the event dressed like a butterfly and ran out on him like Cinderella before the stroke of midnight. But I will give him the benefit of the doubt for now, for your sake." Poppy offered.

Bernice had perked up at the mention of the apparel worn. "I bought a dress that looked like a butterfly for my daughter once. We had a fight and she ran away before she had a chance to wear it to the dance."

Poppy wondered what the odds of two butterfly dresses were. Of course, it was not an expensive original and many copies may have been reproduced from the same design back in that day. Misty would probably have been near the age of Bernie's daughter, so the coincidence made more sense. "I should have brought it by for you to see Bernie, before I dropped it off to be cleaned. Maybe I will before I return it to the owner." Poppy told her.

"Does Jaxon know that you know about me?" Chet returned to the prior subject.

"No, it was such a surprise when I realized he was the son that you have been wanting me to meet, that I didn't know what to say. I wanted to talk to you first to get your side of the story." Poppy answered. "It was sweet of you to think of me for him, Chester, but I am way out of your son's league. Especially if he knew my living circumstances."

"Things are not always exactly how they often appear. I think your living circumstances may be just what he needs to find balance in his life." Chet told her.

"Did you think he was handsome?" Bernie threw in some girl talk.

"Chester Jaxon Cohen is very nice looking and intelligent and quite the catch. Just like his dashing father. You should have seen all the women trying to fathom how I was there with him." Poppy mused. "That part was especially enjoyable."

"Maybe I am not such a bad matchmaker after all. I had a feeling you two might hit it off. These things can take time." Chet smiled. "I won't give up you know."

"If you ever speak with him, let me know what he has to say about me." Poppy suggested. "In the meantime, keep your expectations low."

"It is not likely I will speak with him, but who knows what can happen." Chet was cryptic.

"I say expect the unexpected" Bernie added looking into Poppy's eyes. "If you ever come across my Mistaya May, be good to her too. Take her under those gossamer wings of yours."

Mistaya? The name was eerily close to Misty. And Poppy was not in the position to be of much help to anyone else these days. Just keeping her grandmother safe and cared for was draining her funds, along with her emotional bank account. "I will wish for your daughter on all of the falling stars we sleep under and pray to those Star People like the Lakota did in their legend." Or to any other God that may be up there watching over us, she thought. "That's about the best I have to offer, Bernie."

Usually Poppy left her visits with the shelter-deprived duo in singing spirits, but today her heart and mind were heavy as she walked away, acutely aware of her limitations

Poppy made an effort to hug her grandmother every opportunity she got. She worried about how few hugs were left between the two of them. There was still time today to

go by and collect one before she had to be at work, so she headed to Greener Pastures.

G-ma Daisy's eyes had a glazed-over look when Poppy entered her room. Poppy knew from experience that today was going to be a non-verbal visit. Her grandmother's mind was in another place at the moment and if Poppy pushed too hard, the glaze would turn to one of frantic panic looking back at her. Instead she sat down softly on the edge of the bed, laced her fingers alternately through the blue-veined ones and soothingly shared a fairytale remix with Poppy-ella as the main character.

"Once upon a time there was a young woman named Poppy-ella, not Cinder-Poppy because she did not sleep by the fireplace cinders but slept anyplace she could find. Her parents had also passed away, like the original Ella's. However, instead of a cruel step-mother, she was raised by a kind-hearted grandmother, who unfortunately at this juncture of our tale, could rarely remember her. Poppy-ella's playmates were not white mice, but human homeless dwellers and library workers. Her fairy godmother may not be magical, but maybe more Misty-cal. Poppy-ella did not sweep, scrub, cook and clean like Cinderella, but she did toil to survive in her own way and realm.

134

One day she was invited by the prince himself to a library board ball. Poppy-ella did not feel worthy to go to the party amid all the rich and well-known in their library kingdom and she had nothing to wear to such a fancy affair. But her Misty-cal fairy godmother turned her into a butterfly with wings and she was driven to the ball in the prince's chariot.

Poppy-ella felt like a princess while she was there. She did not dance with the prince, but swirled around the room with him, ate fine cakes and was a part of his important presentation. Before the strike of midnight, Poppy-ella knew she had to leave lest the prince find out she was not a princess, but a humble homeless flower.

Poppy-ella escaped before the prince found out she had no home to be taken too. Unable to retrieve a glass slipper, the prince charming in this version of the story, will have to locate his vanished date by following the trail to Poppy-ella's place of employment…. should he ever want to reconnect with her or take her back to his kingdom again." Poppy paused.

"Oh grandma, I could really use some matriarchal counsel right now. I know it is not your fault that you're not a hundred percent here for me. I am sure you would prefer to be mentally aware, if you had the choice, and I do appreciate having your physical self to hold onto. I cannot go to Chet with this dilemma since the prince happens to be his not-so-doting son. Then with Russell, it would be a conflict of interest. I am semi-conflicted in whom I am interested in. It does not seem kosher to ask one man about a possible relationship with another. That would be mean-girl tacky."

Poppy saw Mona peer into G-ma Daisy's room as she walked past the open doorway. From the look on Mona's face, Poppy surmised Mona knew that Poppy, also known as Poppy-ella, was the snitch. Well, why not add another awkward interchange to her growing file of them. Poppy had no regrets with this one. All developing stories need a good villain anyway. Considering how few tangible items she possessed, it was of utmost importance to Poppy to be able to live well with the things she carried inside herself. She was the only person who had to live with herself.

It was nearly time to take off for her shift at the library. Poppy planned to stay after work to study and complete homework for her classes, then conveniently fall asleep there for the night. She kissed Grandma Daisy's forehead goodbye, wondering if she should lock the door on the way out. Poppy was not sure of the best way to keep an antagonist from accomplishing their nefarious intentions, whether in her adapted story or real life.

CHAPTER 12

Texas, California and Florida have the
highest numbers of unaccompanied homeless
youth under the age of 18, comprising 58%
of the total homeless under 18 youth
population. About half of the youth on the
street report that their parents knew they
were leaving but didn't care. There is
actually an entire generation of homeless
Japanese youths who live and sleep in
internet cafes.

Moriah Bengal found Poppy sleeping draped over a keyboard the next morning. Exhausted from all the emotions of the last few days, she had not even made it upstairs to the couch...a blessing in disguise. The incident appeared to be a simple mistake and not a premeditated sleeping arrangement. However, The Tigress still put Poppy on probation. Somewhere in that woman's body had to be a tiny beating heart, even if her compassion level could lead one to believe she may be a cyborg or modern medical heartless miracle.

Moriah suggested Poppy go get some real sleep, freshen up, and not let it happen again. If the Tigress ever received a deep cut, Poppy was pretty sure ice water would drip from her veins. She thanked Ms. Bengal and left grateful to not be permanently let go.

To prevent being in ill graces with another co-worker, Poppy picked up the precious dry-cleaning package to return it to its rightful owner. She now had a free day to fill.

The tucked-back bungalow remained quiet when Poppy knocked. Misty did not come to the splintery door. There was not a car out front, but Poppy wasn't sure if Misty even drove a car or if she took public transportation. Poppy had no desire to continue carrying the cellophane wrapped garment around town with her and did not feel comfortable leaving it on the crumbling porch for the neighborhood to see. Misty wouldn't care if she left the dress just inside the door, would she?

The front door was locked, but around back Poppy found access through an eight paned glass door. The grout around each glass pane had dried out and was cracked or missing in several spots. One of the small squares of glass was loose and Poppy was able to slide out the single square, reach in and turn the door handle from inside. Then she replaced the pane in its tenuous position, hoping it would not fall out and shatter.

As she set the dress down, Poppy had an overwhelming desire to take another look into the butterfly room. She would be extremely careful not to let any of the insects out. Calling to Misty to make sure there were no surprises, she tiptoed down the short hall past two doors, one the bathroom she changed in on her last visit and the other must be Misty's bedroom. She would not violate her fairy godmother's privacy by peeking in where she had not been invited before, so continued through the living room and barely cracked opened the portal to see into the mock rainforest of colorful wings.

The irresistible insects drew her through the slit until she was once again sitting on the floor in the midst of them. Poppy would be content to while-away her day in this very spot. Maybe she should put on the dress and become one of them…a large Lycaena big sister who hopefully would not end up pinned on the walls. They could flock to her and form a humanoid kaleidoscope. The delicate creatures circled and swooped around the room wispily buzzing her head. If she shut her eyes she could hear their fragile wings beating, but she did not want to miss the visual beauty for more than a few moments.

Poppy knew she should slip out of the butterfly room, but something inside kept prodding her to stay. With her luck, she would be arrested for breaking and entering. She could get a criminal record, but on the bright side, gain a place to live in the process, even if it was behind bars... interesting trade off, she mused to herself.

She noticed the double doors which had caused Misty discomfort when Poppy asked about them earlier. Poppy would not go through them into wherever they went, but merely sneak a quick glance before she headed home...or she should say, headed off. Curiosity was getting the better of her, she was becoming a hard-core snoop.

Partially pulling open one half of the wooden set, Poppy could not have imagined anything close to what she saw before her, even with her fairly vivid imagination. The space reminded her of Harry Potter's living quarters under the stairs, if Harry's space had been decorated in minimalist medical torture chamber decor. The opening was not a room, but a large closet. A single lightbulb with pull string was dangling from the ceiling. A makeshift bed, probably originally a shelf, jutted out from the back wall and filled most of the area. The ledge was covered with a foam pad, sheets and topped with a lemony yellow and brown quilt. The underside was soft minky yellow, with a coarser brown material on the back or alternate side.

The element that made absolutely no sense, was what Poppy saw lying on the shelf-bed between the sheets. A young girl, preteen or early teen, it was hard to tell, was sleeping or resting tucked in the closet. Her eyes were shut, long dark lashes fanned out above her cheeks and soft dishwater blonde curls framed her pale face. The child did not look malnourished, she was more like a young version of Snow White or Sleeping Beauty. An IV drip line hung at the head of the makeshift bed and tubing carried some kind of fluid into her slender arm which was strapped to the shelf by a leather cuff. It must not be simply sugar water from the length of the complicated words on the plastic bottle and the overall health of the recipient.

The girl was clothed in a cross between a simple homemade shift and hospital gown made out of butterfly fabric. Her finger and toenails were painted sky blue with butterfly appliqués on several of the individual nails. Whomever this small person was, she was loved and tended too. Albeit in a horror story sort of way.

This must be Poppy's punishment for prying where she didn't belong. Wait. What a self-absorbed thought. The small body lying in front of her was in a far more precarious position than Poppy. Hesitant to touch the girl's skin and feel for a pulse, Poppy placed her hand below the nostrils of the supine figure. She could feel warm puffs air arising at regular intervals. At least she wasn't dealing with a corpse.

The girl seemed vaguely familiar. Could Poppy have seen her on a missing children's poster at the library? Had Misty kidnapped the girl? Then it hit Poppy where she had seen a similar face. In Misty's living room. Though the girl in the photos was several years younger, the resemblance was undeniable. This must be Misty's daughter Aporia and there must be a logical explanation. Maybe Aporia was in a coma and Misty could not afford health care, but why keep her in the closet? Unless, Misty was the one keeping her daughter in a coma for some unfathomable reason.

Poppy was frozen to the spot. She had absolutely no idea what she should do. She did not have to wonder long. A non-human noise, perhaps the sound a butterfly would make if they had a sound, erupted from behind her. Poppy turned to see Misty gaping at her with eyes and mouth both wide open. The shrill run-on sentence, "*whathaveyoudone?*" dribbled from Misty's open mouth. "She is in her cocoon state and must not be disturbed at this stage of development." Misty howled.

This situation was light years away from a normal, healthy mother/daughter relationship. Poppy needed to use major finesse to not agitate Misty even more. Lilac may not have been nominated for mother of the year, but Poppy had never been condemned to a closest. Striving for understanding, Poppy delved gently, "Misty, is this your Aporia? Is she sick?"

"Of course, this is my beloved Aporia. She is not sick, but perfect." Misty replied.

"Then help me Misty. I know I crossed major boundaries by being in here. I am very sorry. I was just returning your dress and got carried away. But please, why is your daughter in this closet with an IV in her arm? Did you do this?" Poppy held back the scream that was trapped in her throat.

"Don't worry Poppy. I am keeping her in a protective state. Shielding her from the evils of the world until she is ready." Misty reasoned unreasonably.

"What are you saving her from?" Poppy had firsthand knowledge this world could be hard and unfair but wanted clarification from Misty's perspective.

"A man will never do to Aporia what he did to me. She will remain in her chrysalis until she has grown to a butterfly and is old enough to fly away if a predator comes after her." Misty answered.

145

Poppy had a pretty good idea what a man *did* to Misty, but still needed inspiration to help this hideous mess. "You are protecting Aporia from unwanted advances? How old is she? Or how long has she been *cocooned* and how long do you need to keep her in here?" Poppy inquired as calmly as she could. She would start with basic facts.

"Aporia Mae will turn fourteen at the end of this summer. Last year she became a woman. Women of the Tudor time period would say her monthly 'flowers' began. I was seventeen when I was deflowered. I have to keep her safe. I must keep my precious Aporia hidden and cocooned until she is an adult, legally and mentally, probably until she's twenty-one." Misty matter-of-factly responded, like she was sending her daughter off to camp.

Poppy's mental math calculated that meant Aporia would not see the light of day for seven more years. Teen years were difficult, but no young person should have to miss them all. Talk about going to need therapy…. for all three of the women in this room. "Misty, I know you want to be a good mother and take the best care of Aporia that you can, but do you think this might be a bit extreme?" Poppy needed to stall to think of what to do. "Can you give me an idea of what happened to you, Misty? I am so sorry, I want to understand, I truly do."

Misty looked around the room at all the butterflies flying and pinned. Her expression morphed into something almost childlike as she began telling her story. "I was going to be a butterfly and wear my dress. Mark said he loved me. He was taking me to our prom. He wanted to show me how much he would love me forever. Then he hurt me. When I told my mother, she was so angry. She shouted at me and called me names. She worried what the neighbors would think...a grand-baby out of wedlock. I ran away. I had Aporia in a woman's shelter. We are all each other has. I won't be my mother. I don't want Aporia to get hurt. I don't want her to run away. She has to be safe." Misty gave the Reader's Digest version of her last fourteen years in a detached, clipped speech pattern.

Misty's Mark had not only physically assaulted her, but mentally maimed her in the act. Poppy could not leave this situation to a Director Metcalfe-type solution and watch and wait to see how things worked out. Before her was painted a glaring example that not all homes are wonderful. It took more than a roof over one's head to have a safe space. Poppy had become the recipient of another secret, but this one she must act on immediately. "Misty, you have to know this is not okay. You cannot leave Aporia in the closet. There are other ways to protect her."

"GET OUT…NOW…get out!" Misty raged as she shoved Poppy towards the door. "You do not know what you are saying. I should never have let you come here. I even let you wear the dress."

Poppy backed towards the door while repeating gently, "It will be okay, it will be okay, it will be okay." Not really sure if she was talking to Misty or herself. Once outside, Poppy heard the lock bolted shut. Forced violence would not have benefitted Aporia. Fear fluttered in her heart, Poppy had no idea what Misty was capable of. She had to call for backup. Was this a matter for the police, or child services, or should she call an ambulance? Poppy sat on the steps and pressed the numbers 911 on her track phone, which she kept only for emergencies. If this was not an emergency what was? She would wait as sentinel and see who arrived to sort out the situation and save the girl.

CHAPTER 13

Tens of thousands of veterans are homeless.
Over 57,000 veterans are homeless each
night, according to HUD. Sixty percent of
them are in shelters, the rest unsheltered.
Just over 8 percent or nearly 5,000 of
homeless U.S. veterans are female.

The cavalry arrived. Two vehicles with flashing lights drove through the vacant lot to park with their bumpers pressed up to the porch where Poppy waited. Two more plain cars arrived on the scene moments later. The flowers on each side of where she sat were barely spared a smashing. Funny that she felt worried for the flowers when a human life was hanging in the balance inside.

The next few minutes seemed like something out of a B movie or poorly written novel. Poppy gave the officers the bare facts as she knew them, they forced entry, cuffed a hysterical Misty and placed the sleeping beauty Aporia in an ambulance. Now Poppy really realized what she had done. Dr. Metcalfe might have construed a more humane plan. The betrayal in Misty's eyes as she was folded into the police car haunted Poppy. Her housing circumstances may not be the only reason she had trouble keeping friends.

The police requested Poppy come in for questioning, so she followed with the child services representative in an older model four door sedan. Poppy could feel the springs through the back seat and dwelt on how many others had sat in this exact spot. She felt sick. "Excuse me, could you tell me what is going to happen to my friend? More like acquaintance? The mother? I didn't want to get her in trouble, just make sure her daughter was okay." Poppy directed her question to the woman driving the car.

"It is hard to say at this point. Many things will be taken into consideration. For instance, did she have criminal intent? My best guess it that she will be admitted to a mental hospital to get the help she needs for now and the courts will decide where she belongs later."

"How about her daughter? Aporia?" Poppy asked.

"She will be evaluated at a medical hospital while we attempt to locate other family members. Do you know her family?" the unnamed woman asked.

"I don't think so." Poppy was not about to divulge more information at this point until she thought things through more carefully. The Bernie connection could be coincidence and she did not want to implicate another friend.

The rest of the ride took place in silence. There was not even the radio to defuse the starkness and distract her mind. This would not end up being a 'rest and freshen up' day as Moriah had suggested. Poppy was led to an office where she waited between visits and interrogations from different agencies. Poppy began to feel like she was the one who was guilty.

After several hours, Poppy was given an update from the police and a request from CSD…Child Services Division. The arresting officer entered the room first and shared with Poppy, "I wanted you to know that your friend, Mistaya, has been admitted to a mental health facility where she will be evaluated and get the help she needs at this time." The CSD woman was right on.

"Will she have to go to jail?" Poppy worried.

"There is possible prosecution with this case, but not likely. I do not believe this woman is a danger to anyone but herself and daughter," the policeman shared, then added when he saw Poppy's concern. "You did the right thing. Don't feel badly. They are both going to get the help they need. If you hadn't contacted us when you did, we could have been dealing with a homicide instead."

Small consolation. Poppy had ruined another person's life. "What about the butterflies?"

"Not sure what will happen there. This is a first for me. I would suppose they will be donated to the local college science department or maybe an animal preserve or insect museum, if there is such a thing, unless family members claim them. But the perp seemed pretty isolated." Then Officer Platt was out the door. Poppy wished she had a place to keep butterfly room, somewhere safe.

Regina Bozeman, the CSD lady, returned. "It looks like you are our heroine today. The daughter is going to be just fine. Doctors were able to wake her up and there seems to be no permanent physical damage."

"Yeah." Poppy emitted weakly. "I am truly thrilled Aporia is going to be okay, but curious how Misty had the knowledge to do what she did and not cause damage to her daughter. This is such a sick world."

"I agree, it is a pretty crazy place. According to the information we have been able uncover at this point, it appears Misty is an intelligent woman and was able to educate herself online and with library resources on venipuncture and phlebotomy. She procured the needles, tubing and IV bags she needed from a medical supply store in St. Anthony telling them it was for an elderly relative who could not get the nutrition needed by mouth. Misty only administered fluid and nutrition replacement intravenously, no medication, so she would not need a prescription.

To keep Aporia knocked out, Misty acquired a heavy-duty sleeping pill prescription from her own physician. She then crushed and administered doses, intended for a much larger person, twice a day. It is a wonder she did not kill the girl. I guess she asked her doctor originally for Propofol, the drug that killed Michael Jackson. It slows the activity of your brain and nervous system and is used during medical procedures to sedate a patient who is under critical care. Lucky for them both, her doctor was cautious enough to not give it to her or we may be dealing with a much more serious crime." Poppy listened intently to the unimaginable.

Regina continued, "Our main concern now is what to do with Aporia once she is stable and free to leave the hospital. Unfortunately, we have been unable to locate any family members at this point. I wondered, while we are waiting for permanent placement, if you might be interested in taking the girl home for a few days? You seem to have a vested interest and would be given resources."

This may be the absolute worst Poppy had ever felt about not having a home to go home to. Dragging Aporia around with her to her surprise sleeping-spot-for-the-night would doubtfully aid in recovery. Sunny-mobile had bucket seats in the front, so was not conducive to double bunking and the rest of her locations were not exactly private residences. Poppy could make up excuses and avoid direct confrontation of the facts, as per her usual plan, but she was tired today. She had heard confession was good for the soul.

"Ms. Bozeman, I would actually love to take Aporia home with me, but the problem is…and I would ask that you please keep this to yourself, I am sure there is some confidentiality clause with the people you deal with…I, myself, do not actually have a home to go home to, in the traditional sense of the word. I do fine and make do, but it would not really be a viable option for anyone's recuperation." Poppy felt an odd relief at stating the facts out loud.

"I have another suggestion though. I have two friends with accommodations that would be appropriate, and I would be willing to stay at either location with Aporia until she had a place to go. I could check with them and get back to you soon?" Poppy offered.

She thought of Xavier Max's huge home and how hospitable he had been when she was dropped off at his doorstep unexpectedly. Poppy was pretty sure they would be welcome there for a few days. Then she could always count on Russell. Poppy knew he would give up his own room, and even the very shirt off his back, if he did not have extra room. He would do everything in his power to make sure she and whomever else she requested sanctuary for, were taken care of. She did have plausible options.

Regina Bozeman was quiet for a moment, probably digesting the information and options she had just been fed Poppy guessed. "I will get back to you on that Poppy. Thank you for your willingness, but hopefully you will not have to ask your friends. They have not been vetted. I am sure there are others in the system who will work just fine. I just wanted to give you the option first, you are the closest thing we have to 'family' currently." In reality Regina Bozeman was thinking, if Poppy were a little younger, she would add her to her case load and find a home for her as well.

Poppy was released to go, but CSD and the police both asked that she checkback in the morning, in case they decided to use her housing options for Aporia and also for any further questions or information updates. As she left the police station, Poppy was not sure which way to turn. Should she go share with Bernie the possible family drama? No, she was too tired. It had been a very long day after her keyboard-pillow night. And what would she tell her? I think you might be the mother of my Misty. Are you the mother whose angry words caused her to run away, have a baby on her own and eventually drug and cocoon your grandchild? Nope, she was not ready for that discussion.

She could go gain solace from her grandma, but she preferred someone who actually responded logically or at least heard what she was saying. Jaxon Cohen might be able to help, but she had not spoken with him since the Cinderella episode and did not know where he lived. His high tax bracket house was certainly across town.

That left Russell. Some people had comfort foods they went to in times of stress. Poppy had a comfort person. She did not really want to go back inside the library, but she would wait for him outside. She was sure Russell would be working with both she and Misty indisposed. It was getting late, he should be off soon. She waited on a bench out front near the bottom of the ramp so not to miss him.

Within the hour, her wheelchair warrior rolled down the ramp. A smile lit his face when he saw Poppy. "Poppet, what a pleasant surprise."

"I am sure you must have heard." She simply said.

"I assume you mean about Misty?" Russell asked.

"Yes, butterfly loving, secret life living, Misty." Poppy droned.

"Not really. When she did not show up for work today, The Tigress tried to call her, but got no answer. She eventually called the local police, since Misty never misses and is always reliable. Mariah said she did not want to wait twenty-four hours in case there had been foul play. She must watch Dateline or 20/20. All they told her was that Misty was taken into custody. I assume you know more?" Russell inquired.

"Much more than I ever wanted to know." Poppy proceeded to fill Russell in on all the gory details of her day. He let Poppy pour it all out, without interrupting with the million questions in his mind.

When Poppy finished or at least paused for intermission, Russell interjected. "Golly gee whiz girl, you have had quite the day, almost unbelievable. Our co-worker's butterfly addiction was always a little weird, but we all have our quirks. Who would have guessed there was so much more going on behind Misty's closed doors, literally? It is almost a miracle you found that poor girl. Pretty fortuitous you returned the dress and are so curious by nature." Russell gave the depleted Poppy a little pep talk.

"You are generous my friend. I suppose that is why I told you." Poppy was grateful she had.

"Just honest." Russell said.

"I really don't want to be alone tonight and…. I know you have offered before…." Poppy had parted ways with her pride eons ago, but hesitated asking straight out.

"Yes, you are welcome to stay at my home tonight." Russell replied without her having to finish the sentence.

"On one condition," Poppy said. "I refuse to kick you out of your bed. Your couch would be more than fine."

"That will be contrary to my gentlemanly inclinations, but I will see what I can do." Russell jested.

Poppy threw her arms around Russell's neck and landed a peck on his cheek. When the action she felt more inclined to do, was to drop down and sit in his lap and let Russell roll her wherever he was going. She was suddenly totally and completely exhausted. "I have faith in you." Poppy encouraged. "And one more thing, is there any way we can swing by a drive-in restaurant on the way. I am famished."

"I can do better than that. I will whip you up some famous Redmond grub at the old homestead. You look like you could use more nutrition than a fast food meal would supply." Russell realized he may get his opportunity to impress the girl after-all. Victory goes to the slow and steady.

Poppy followed Russell back behind the library to the parking lot, not to the bus stop. For some reason she had just assumed he took public transportation. She was wrong, there in a handicapped parking space was a decked-out pickup truck, with chairlift, that enabled Russell to drive his own vehicle from his wheelchair using hand controls. The man never ceased to amaze her.

"You are a man of many wonders." Poppy was impressed.

"You have no idea all I have up my sleeve." Russell quipped as he whipped the monster truck out of its parking stall and drove the damsel in distress home to his castle.

It would be the first day in forever that Poppy would not make it to Greener Pastures. Under the circumstances, she was sure her grandmother would understand. If G-ma

Daisy understood or noticed her absence at all. To be totally honest, their visits were more for Poppy.

CHAPTER 14

Domestic violence is a leading cause of homelessness among women. According to the National Law Center on Homelessness and Poverty (NLCHP), more than 90 percent of homeless women are victims of severe physical or sexual abuse, and escaping that abuse is a leading cause of their homelessness.

Russell unintentionally woke Poppy upon entering his living room the next morning. The previous evening, he fed her pasta with pesto and a fresh green salad. He had put her to bed on his sofa with a full stomach, where she dropped almost instantly into a dead sleep for ten solid hours.

Poppy was dreaming, about a land with flowers that spoke, as he walked in. The petalled plants were of all colors and varieties. They did not need frame-built houses. Some grew under trees for shelter and others preferred direct sunlight overhead. The idea of homelessness was ludicrous in their land. A few members of the flower community were worried about an influx of butterflies from a neighboring village, while others spoke out that they should all welcome the insects and live in harmony. The latter group offered to share their petals as resting pads for the beautiful winged creatures.

Poppy was roused from her dreamland travels just as the flowers where putting to a vote how to handle the butterfly invasion. Were they to be their friends or foes? As she opened her eyes, she saw Russell observing her from across the room, not wanting to disturb her. She must have felt his presence subconsciously. Too bad she could not stay asleep and invite him to join her in the land of flower dreams instead. She should be embarrassed to have invited herself to invade his private space, but she felt refreshed. It was the first good rest she had had in ages.

"Would you like some breakfast sleepyhead?" Russell offered.

"Maybe something quick, if it's not a bother. I am scheduled to work later this morning." Poppy reminded herself vocally. "And if it is not too extremely awkward, what I would really adore is a shower?" She was making herself right at home, but it somehow seemed okay with Russell.

"You are welcome to whatever you need. I can drive you in to work if you would like." Russell was going to make the most of the time he had with Poppy here "You can even come back after work tonight, to do homework or whatever, if you would like to that is." Was he trying too hard?

"Thanks Russell. We will see. I should really get by to see my grandmother and I have an Xavier book exchange to fit in today too. But I appreciate the offer immensely." Poppy grabbed her backpack and headed to the bathroom to actually freshen up as Moriah Bengal had suggested twenty-four hours ago.

Had it only been twenty-four hours? It seemed like a week since her discovery of Aporia and ensuing confrontation with Misty. She needed to check in with the police and CSD before the day ended as well. Her dance card was getting full. Hopefully Russell's retreat would fuel Poppy with the sustenance and shut-eye required to face the ensuing onslaught. It would be easy to stay here indefinitely, but that would be not fair to Russell until she deciphered her feelings for him.

His place had a definite vibe to it. What was it...minimalist? The decor was spare, nothing hung on the walls and the furniture was sparse with simple lines. Russell had only what he needed, leaving room for him to wheel around. The only busy energy she felt at all came from his fortress of books. A built-in bookcase went half

163

way up the wall, surrounding the room on three sides. The furniture had been moved to the middle. Last night she must have been too tired to take notice.

Water from the shower washed away the last bit of her grogginess and yogurt with toast filled her morning emptiness. Poppy could get used to this. With a woman's touch Russell's apartment would be a perfect haven. A distinct impression permeated her, she may be the only woman who had been inside these walls for some time, unless he had a cleaning woman.

To finish off the five-star stay and service, Poppy let Russell drive her to work. "Thanks for the cowboy limo service in your honkin' huge truck. I won't take advantage of your goodness further, at least for today." Poppy teased.

"I am here at your beck and call Miss Poppy Paisley. Would you like to stop by the police station to check in on the way?"

"Do we have time? I don't want to rile The Tigress by being late when she's short staffed. Perhaps I can just borrow your phone and give them a call? I don't have many minutes on my phone and forgot to charge it last night." Poppy could not stop herself from accepting more when offered.

"You were too busy charging yourself my friend." Russell replied as he tossed Poppy his cell.

Officer Platt answered the call and filled Poppy in on the latest details as he knew them. Misty was safely stashed in the psych wing of the St. Anthony hospital. Her initial evaluation led them to believe she would be moving to a more long-term mental facility soon and legal action of any kind would be postponed to a much later date if ever. Misty was currently not allowed any visitors, but no one had requested visitation. Misty seemed to be settling in and was no longer in a manic state. Poppy was certainly not ready to see her, she still felt like Brutus betraying butterfly Caesar.

Officer Platt did not know what was happening with Aporia but gave Poppy Regina's number at CSD. It was not as easy to get in touch with Regina. Poppy left her a brief message with the library as the return phone number. She wished she was in a position to take the petite girl. Poppy wanted to make sure she ended up in a situation better than closet-living or on a park bench with Bernie, her could-be grandmother.

The library was quiet except for a few reporters attempting to put together a story about the Misty affair. Moriah forbid the staff from speaking with the media on library time, which was fine with Poppy. She did not feel like a heroine, more a butterfly hunter who had tangled Misty in her net. Poppy missed finding the daily butterfly puzzle of the day hidden on her co-worker and hoped she had done the right thing. Every time she pictured Aporia in a drug induced sleep on the shelf, she knew she had.

Poppy decided to use her late lunch break to make the book delivery to Xavier Max, that would free-up more time to spend with her grandma after work. She didn't even look for a bag on Xavier's porch this time but went straight to the door and entered. After spending the night with a person, boundaries changed, she chuckled. Poppy found Xavier in his reading chair book-less and busily plucking away on his laptop.

"Hello, Professor X, hopefully I'm not interrupting anything of grave importance. What are you working on?" Poppy asked her Pillsbury doughboy friend.

"I took your advice Miss Paisley and have begun writing my own book." Xavier admitted.

Pleased she occasionally had good advice at least for others, Poppy exclaimed, "Ooooo, that is so cool. Can you tell me anything about the plot or will I have to wait?"

"I am just unfolding the narrative now. Writing what I know about, a sci-fi story as you suggested, but it will have an element of romance entwined. I plan to have my Zelda character fall in love with one of the Mario Brothers." Xavier shared proudly.

"You never know what book will turn out to be a blockbuster." Poppy told him, thinking to herself, or if one will turn out to be a mad mess. "Do you still want me to bring books by?"

"Of course, the best writers read prolifically. However, I think I will cut my load in half and split the time between reading and typing pages. What have you been up to since out last encounter? Any recent random sleepovers?" Xavier quizzed.

Poppy chose not to share that she had in fact couch-surfed last night at Russell's but did tell Xavier all about the Misty/Aporia mishap before he heard or read about it in the news.

"You do get into some unique scraps Poppy Paisley. Perhaps you are the one who should be writing. Is there anything I can do to help the unfortunate mother and daughter?" Xavier asked.

"Well, CSD was looking for a temporary home for Aporia, but I cannot imagine they would place a young teenage girl with a single middle-aged man, no matter how harmless you are Xavier. I could give them glowing references from my stay here." Poppy smiled. "You do have many unused rooms. You might consider turning one of them into a butterfly sanctuary, if you cannot house the butterfly girl herself. Those insects are going to need a new home too."

"You imagine I am one of those Anniversary Inns, with a different theme for each room one enters? I will ponder on that suggestion. The Max mansion as a habitat, not for wronged humanity, but for the abandoned winged. Your visits always fill my life with excitement dear girl. Don't stay away too long."

She sensed she was being gently dismissed. Xavier was in the writing mode and did not want to lose any of the fresh ideas on his brain. Poppy had to get back to finish her shift at the library anyway. Perhaps a seed had been planted that would hopefully grow fruit in his ample bosom and eventually one of his extra rooms. Xavier was a good man. She was sure he would figure out how to help somehow.

The reporters had evaporated when Poppy returned to work. Jaxon Cohen was waiting for her in their place. He always made her feel like an awkward teen again, if she had ever outgrown that phase. Her face flushed as she recalled their last encounter and her explosive exit from his car.

Jaxon stepped towards her. "I wanted to stop by and see how you are doing. I have been concerned about you since the library event and then heard about your exploits yesterday. It is all over the local news. You have a way of making a lasting impression." He gazed down at the floor. Poppy wished she had an inkling of what he was thinking. His tight, handsome, jawline and hooded, gray-green eyes, gave away no clues.

"Just trying to keep life interesting. *'Causing commotion wherever I go'* is my motto." Poppy piped.

"You are in good spirits I see. I just wanted to make sure I had not offended you in some way and let you know I am available. To assist you I mean. Sorry to bother you." Jaxon looked like he was getting ready to go and Poppy was not ready for him to.

"I don't mean to be abrupt. I feel pretty awful about the whole encounter." Poppy partially pulled off her mask.

Jaxon wondered if she was referring to her recent butterfly release and ensuing escapade or their abruptly ended date. He chose to proceed on the safer route, heading down the less personal and not the potentially thorny path. "Was the woman on the news the co-worker you borrowed the butterfly dress from?" Jaxon asked.

"How did you guess?" Poppy smiled. "I was returning it when I stumbled upon much more than I bargained for."

"Sounds like you were at the right place, at the right time. Rescuing another person without even trying. That reminds me of the other reason I stopped by, to thank you for your support with my project. It looks like we may be able to get the backing needed to go ahead with the library plus plan. I will need to jump through a few more hoops but should know the outcome in the next month or two." Jaxon Cohen got more animated when discussing the library annex. When his face lit up, he looked more like his father, and Poppy remembered she was supposed to be mad at him.

"Yeah, about that project. I have a few questions for you." But instead of confronting C. J. Cohen Jr. about his dad, who already lived in the park, Poppy had another idea come to mind. "What would you think about incorporating a themed room into the annex to tie together the library and housing components?"

"What did you have in mind?" Jaxon asked.

"My thoughts are just in the bud stage, but how about a butterfly room between the two sides? Misty will not be able to tend to her daughter or her specimens for quite some time. She has this amazing collection of butterflies, both living and dead, that are going to need a new home. It seems like they could be symbolic for the homeless. An inspiration that they can go from caterpillars, to grow their own wings and fly. It is probably a kooky idea, but I wanted to put it out there. No pressure, I am working on another option for them as well." Poppy was not sure why she was so worried about the butterflies. Maybe because she could not do anything to help Aporia? Was she transferring her nurturing abilities to a simpler life form? It seemed strange.

"Life is never boring with you around Miss Paisley. I would have to check into the legality and if there is any other party who has interest in the collection, but I promise to look into it."

Jaxon Cohen hunched slightly forward, like he was going in to give Poppy a hug or something, then thought better of it, and stretched out his hand to offer a shake. She clasp his strong smooth hand letting his fingers protectively

171

encircle hers. The traditional exchange suddenly became a very romantic gesture. If just holding this man's hand left her feeling light headed, Poppy wondered what a kiss from those stubble-surrounded lips would be like. Perhaps she was attracted to bad boys.

Jaxon Cohen left the building but did not exit her thoughts. Poppy had so much to share with her grandmother tonight. And freeing a girl from her cocoon may not even be the most captivating topic.

CHAPTER 15

Many people are homeless because they cannot afford rent. HUD has experienced cuts in recent decades, resulting in the loss of 10,000 units of subsidized low-income housing. There are fewer places for poor people to rent than before. According to the NLCHP (National Law Center on Homeless & Poverty), one eighth of the nation's supply of low-income housing has been permanently lost since 2001. Eleven million households now pay more than 50% of their income for housing which is an increase of 20% since 2007. Using their resources creatively to house the poor, the country of Albania having built hundreds of thousands of bunkers under communism, applied a little ingenuity and transformed some of them into housing for their homeless people.

Aporia wanted to talk to Poppy. Regina called the library to let Poppy know and ask that she come by the hospital before Aporia was discharged. In the three days the doctors kept Aporia admitted, copious medical tests were run, but they incredibly found no negative effects from her confinement. CSD found a foster care home in a neighboring city, far enough away to keep the media from preventing Aporia from enjoying a quasi-normal life. Poppy was nervous to see the butterfly she had helped exit her chrysalis too early. She had no idea what to say or expect.

Luckily Regina went into the room with them when Poppy arrived. Aporia was sitting up in bed, no longer wearing her butterfly print gown. The yellow blouse and jeans eliminated some of her fairytale qualities. Aporia may no longer be sleeping beauty, but Misty's daughter was truly a lovely young woman. However, the look on Aporia's face did not convey joy to her rescuer. She looked sad and lost. Perhaps she hadn't had enough time for her metaphorical wings to grow.

"Are you my mom's friend who found me?" Aporia asked.

Poppy was not sure how to answer, she wondered if Misty would consider her a friend at this point. "Hello Aporia, I am the person who discovered you, yes. I am happy you are doing so well."

"My mother was not a bad mom you know. I would be willing to give up another year to have her back." Tears filled Aporia's eyes. "She was just afraid and trying to take care of me."

Was Aporia manifesting that syndrome where a person develops feelings for their kidnapper? No, of course not, Aporia really loved her mother and probably felt she had just been asleep a short time. "I am so sorry Aporia, but you must understand, I could not leave you in that closet. I was not trying to get your mother in trouble but save you."

"I know. It just doesn't feel that way. I want my mom back. I don't want to live with strangers." The liquid blue eyes spilled tears down her cheeks.

"I understand. Hopefully your mother will be well soon. In the meantime, I am trying to find a nice place, for your mom's butterflies to live." Poppy shared.

"I should be grateful. I just feel so alone and wanted to meet you. Thank you for coming by." Aporia looked tiny and tired. "I have one more question that has been stuck in my mind…how exactly does one become a butterfly?"

Poppy was not really sure how to answer the hopefully metaphorical question in a way that might bring some peace to the troubled girl. "I suppose you must want to fly so much that you are willing to give up being a caterpillar."

Poppy would visit Aporia at the foster home, if she was allowed, and bring her some books to read. She did not feel much like the girl's savior, more her condemner to this motherless fate. Poppy knew exactly how that felt. If she could find housing for herself, she would definitely welcome this misplaced butterfly. They could be motherless together.

There was a chill in the air as Poppy left the hospital. The weather was turning, there would not be many more outside-in-the-park overnighters for her in the next few months. She wondered how Chet and Bernie handled the colder weather. Obi-Wan had a built-in fur coat and was more prepared for these frosty nights. She felt like being alone with her thoughts tonight, so Poppy headed to her car. She had not slept in Sunny-mobile most of the summer.

Poppy pulled her grandmother's flowered quilt tighter around her shoulders with just her nose poking out. She liked to keep one of the car windows cracked slightly open for ventilation. It was going to be a cooler fall this year. Brrrr. The chill and humidity crept through the thinning threads of the blanket causing her teeth to chatter. She drew her knees up closer to her chin to keep the heat in. Trying to get a little more comfortable, Poppy rolled to her other side, but the rear seat cushions on her 1999 Honda Civic were just not conducive to a five-star sleep any which way she turned. Having her spine against the back of the seat was definitely the warmer position.

Sounds from the starless night surrounded her. Stray noises used to stress her out, but now were oddly comforting and homey. She could hear a siren shrieking over the distant traffic. Small creatures of some variety scurried around the tires under her car and occasionally padded across the roof above her. A bonk pinged on the metal roof, likely an errant nut from the squirrels she saw in the trees during the dusk light. It must be too cold for crickets. Poppy started counting backwards from one hundred to take her mind off the sounds and help her fall asleep. She should count squirrels instead of sheep she chuckled.

From inaudible human shouts, she deduced a fight must be breaking out in the nearby park. And a chipmunk was trying to squeeze its way through the inch-open car window. This would be a short-sleep night for sure. It was a good thing ghost stories and bedding down in a cemetery did not freak her out or she would never be able to shut her eyes and sleep here.

The sirens got closer as the commotion in the adjoining property increased in volume. Poppy put her pillow, which from the smell could use a wash, over her head to drown out the noise. She hoped Chet and Bernie weren't involved, but they were seasoned enough to make themselves scarce if there was a problem. She would check on them in the morning. Fifty-nine, fifty-eight, fifty-seven.

A sudden rap on the window startled her as she was beginning to dose off. Poppy hesitantly withdrew her pillow-muffle to find a flashlight shining blindingly into her eyes. When her pupils adjusted enough to make out an image, she saw one of St. Anthony's finest, a uniformed police officer with badge, was peering through the fogged back passenger window into her makeshift boudoir. Officer Platt had discovered her not-so-mobile home.

"Miss Paisley?!" Surprise plastered Officer Platt's face and Poppy was pretty sure that policemen were not surprised easily. "What are you doing here? No wonder you did not want to bring the cocooned girl home with you."

"Yah, not sure a bucket seat would be a step up from a shelf." Poppy answered dryly.

"There has been an altercation in the park. A homeless man was badly beaten, and we are looking for the fugitive who did it. Have you heard anything, or anyone pass by?" Officer Platt interrogated.

"Just some busy squirrels or what sounded like rodents of some sort." Poppy replied.

"Well, it is not safe for you to stay here tonight. Do you have a place you can go? Or I can find a temporary shelter for you." The officer offered.

"I always scrounge someplace up. Don't worry about me. I hope you find your guy." Poppy said.

"In this community it is difficult to uncover the perpetrator. The homeless camp is extremely tight lipped. I better keep searching. Be safe now!" And Officer Platt was off.

"We better quit meeting like this." Poppy called to his retreating back. The officer turned and gave her a parting smile.

Poppy wondered what had happened over in the park. Chet and Bernie were there. She was not comfortable seeking her own comfort until she made sure they were both okay. The bad guy was long gone anyway, right?

She wrapped her grandma's quilt tighter around her shoulders, making it into a gigantic shawl or maybe more an Indian chief's blanket, and headed down the path to the park. She knew the way well enough she could travel it with ease in the dark. The sounds increased in volume the closer she got, and she could see flashing lights through the trees.

Poppy was not oblivious to the indelicate and often downright dark situations of the homeless plight, yet she often chose to look beyond or above them. She did want to dwell on the negative lest it consume her. However, tonight it was almost impossible to miss what surrounded her as she searched for her friends. In the shadows, ugliness starred her in the face, unsettled her stomach and pinched her heart.

Under a weeping willow tree, she saw a family of four huddled together against the cold. One of the young children was scrawny enough to be buttoned together with his mother against her chest beneath her tattered coat. Grayness reflected from all of their faces in the moonlit night. Near the forlorn family, an older person, Poppy was not sure if they were male or female, attempted to set up some form of shelter in a large cardboard box. At least she had her much more-snug, mostly metal car when needed. It may not be preferred housing but was far better than what these poor people had available to turn to.

Not much further on, behind a few foul-smelling garbage cans that lined a portion of the asphalt path, a man who appeared anywhere between twenty and forty was shooting up. An obviously reused needle hovered above his filthy arm which was tied off with a rubber hose to elevate the engorged welcoming vein. Infection, if not HIV, was knocking on this unfortunate fellow's door. Poppy shuddered as she continued looking.

Finally arriving at the desired destination, Poppy immediately noticed that Chet, Bernie and Obi-wan were not in their normal camping spot. She pushed past, working her way closer to the nucleus of the action. Laying on the ground about two hundred yards from *their bench* was a male figure. His head was heavily bloodied and there seemed to be red fluid seeping from his chest wall as well. The man looked much younger than Chet and was not as dapperly dressed. Poppy breathed out a slow sigh of relief and then felt guilty she was relieved. This severely injured stranger had others who cared about him too and it looked like he may not make it.

"What happened?" Poppy asked the observer closest to her. She noticed a police office, probably Officer Platt's partner, was keeping the crowd at bay as they waited for medical personnel to arrive. Emergency services were not as rapidly acquired by the homeless.

"A couple guys got into a fight. One pulled a knife. I think it was over some possession and there was alcohol involved." A non-injured, standing stranger shared.

"Of course, there was alcohol involved and what possessions do they really have to fight over?" Poppy's mind was racing. The booze would at least dull the pain and the cold would slow the bleeding. Maybe the guy had a chance. But where were Chet and Bernie? Hopefully Chet had not been on the other end of the disagreement. That would be highly unlikely, he was such a gentleman. Poppy could not help worrying about her missing friends. Homeless scatter when there is trouble, but where would they go?

Maybe it was time to confront Jaxon Cohen about his namesake. Her phone was charged and a missing person in the middle of a battle scene was definitely another emergency. She pulled from her backpack the paper with younger Mr. Cohen's cell number on it. He had given it to her earlier when she was searching for the library document. Did she dare dial the number? Did she just like to stir the pot and create drama?

No, this was a son's concern too. It was about time he stepped up and took some responsibility for his dad. It was disgraceful he let his father live in such precarious conditions. With winter on its way maybe Jaxon could find other accommodations for Chet and maybe even Bernie and their dog.

She wondered if there was a Mrs. Chester somewhere in this dysfunctional family picture, but it was not the time to digress on that tangent now. Poppy boldly pounded the ten numbers that would connect her with the prodigal son.

A drowsy "hello" came across the cyberspace phone waves. Oh good, Poppy was glad she had woken him. Why should he get to sleep in a nice warm bed when his father went without?

"Mr. Cohen, this is Poppy Paisley."

"Poppy? Is there a library emergency of some sort?" Jaxon asked bewildered.

"Not exactly, but there is a humanity emergency. There has been a beating in the park. It is a blessing that it does not happen to be your father. But he is missing, I cannot find him anywhere. I thought you should know. In case you had any drop of compassion for the man who sired you." Poppy spewed out with venom.

"Poppy I am not sure what you are talking about. My father is dead." Jaxon somberly replied.

"Well, maybe dead to you Mr. Important Man." Poppy could not thaw the icy shards in her voice. "But let me assure you, your father is very alive and well, living in the St. Anthony City Park."

"I am sorry, but you must be mistaken." Jaxon's voice was flat. "We put my father's very deceased body in a coffin and buried him in the cemetery adjacent to that park over eight years ago." There was silence on the other end of the line. Before she could come up with a response to that unexpected turn in the conversation, Poppy's phone call was dropped and the connection between them went dead as well.

CHAPTER 16

Severe mental illness affects one in five homeless people, but only 6% of the general population, according to government studies. Half of this homeless population self-medicate and are at further risk for addiction and poor physical health. A University of Pennsylvania study tracking nearly 5,000 homeless people for two years discovered that investing in comprehensive health support and treatment of physical and mental illnesses is less costly than incarceration, shelter and hospital services for the untreated homeless.

The sounds and sites of the night blurred. Could images seen with one's own eyes and believed to be truth, in actuality be faulty? Did Chester have a twin brother or doppleganger who assumed his identity like on reruns of the *Arrested Development* television show? Were Bernie and Obi-Wan-Kenobi alive or dead? Poppy's brain felt like it was going to explode. She wished her phone had internet. Two-twelve A.M. flashed across the digital screen. Other sources of access to information would not be open this early, or late, depending on the day.

Still wrapped in the quilt, Poppy sat down on the park bench where she had spent so many moments with the trio in question. She would wait to see it they returned. In her own weird way, she was paying tribute to them and the nights they all spent here together. She did not feel the cold any longer. Poppy felt numb.

The sun rose slowly in a scarlet sky...*red sky at night sailors' delight, red in the morning sailors take warning*...the ditty seemed appropriate for her not-so-smooth sailing. Poppy was not sure if she dosed at all during the night or had just zoned out, but her homeless friends had not returned.

She trudged back to her vehicular home base, swapped out supplies and headed to the YMCA. This morning she would use one of her pass punches and be at the library as soon as the doors opened to begin her research. If she had a key, she would have risked Moriah's wrath and gone last night. She needed to know if Jaxon Cohen was indeed telling the truth and if so, how could that be possible.

At nine o'clock sharp Poppy burst through the library doors and headed to a computer screen. As she buzzed past, Moriah reminded Poppy that she was not scheduled to work yet. Not slowing down, over her shoulder, Poppy informed her boss she had other studies to take care of before her shift began.

She logged onto the computer as rapidly as possible with trembling fingers and slow library connections. Into the search bar she typed Chester's full name. The first item to pop up on the top of the page was his obituary. Poppy didn't even want to open it. There could be fake news on the internet. She scrolled down the page. There were links to Cohen Construction Company along with newspaper articles with a wide range of titles that included his name.

One that set off alarms in her brain was entitled Construction Mogul Found Frozen. Poppy doubted they were reporting that Chet decided to try cryogenics. Fearing what she would find, Poppy accessed the link. The opening paragraph blazed into her eyeballs...*Chester J. Cohen, well known in this community for starting Cohen Construction and for many acts of humanitarian service, has been found dead in St. Anthony City Park. He appears to have frozen to death during an unprecedented cold snap in the weather. Also found deceased in near vicinity to Mr. Cohen, were a female whose name is being withheld until family can be located and notified, and an unidentified dog. Foul play does not seem to be a factor.*

Poppy stopped reading when the article began describing the economic downturn and demise of Cohen Construction. She sat stunned. This made absolutely no sense. Could it be an elaborate hoax of some kind? The date on the article indicated it was written November 24, 2009.... nearly nine years ago.

In Poppy's estimation, hard copies of information could be trusted to be more valid. Leaving the computer, she rushed to the periodical section. Leafing through old newspapers, she found the week she was looking for. There it was over and over again in bold black and white print. Chester found dead, Chester's obituary, Chester buried in the St. Anthony Cemetery. He could even be lying near her mother. There was a follow up article identifying the deceased woman as a Bernice Abernathy, but no family members had come forth. The dog appeared to be a stray.

Poppy slid down to the floor. Her mind was having trouble processing the words she read. She didn't believe that she was mentally ill, but of course if she were mentally off balance, she would be the last person to recognize the fact.

She owed Jaxon Cohen an apology. She had called him out, verbally berated him and mentally convicted him for committing an indecent act created only in her delusion.

What should she do? Where should she go? How had she seen Chet, Bernice and Obi-Wan? They seemed so real. They were real. They walked and talked and gave advice. Then so did imaginary people in psychotic episodes. But why would she have made these exact people up in her mind? There was something she was missing. Poppy just wanted to go lie in a bed next to her grandmother Daisy. She could pull the covers over her head and think things through in her bizarre brain.

Russell rolled up to find her heaped on the floor. Concern etched on his face. "Poppy, what on earth? You don't appear to be okay. Would you like to go rest at my house or do you need to see a doctor?" His words rolled out too.

Poppy probably did need to see a doctor, not a medical one, more likely a shrink. But she was not ready to share, just yet, with her best work bud that she had gone stark raving mad. Perhaps Russell wasn't real either. "I think I just stood up too quickly and haven't had breakfast. I will be fine. Thanks Russ...ell." She wanted to call him Russ or Rusty, but neither seemed to fit. This was not a time for nicknaming. She was just attempting to cement their bond in some way, as Poppy may need his non-deluded perspective in the near future.

"I don't work for a few hours yet, I'll go get some fresh air and a bite to eat and be back much better, before you know it." Poppy decided to go back to the cemetery and see with her own eyes if what she read was for real. "Could you cover for me, if I am a bit late? I need to stop by the cemetery too."

"Are you going to see your mother?" Russell wondered if Poppy's mom, even though no longer living, could offer some kind of support that he, who was right in front of her, could not.

"Maybe a quick visit, but there is another grave I need to locate, a person I just found out is dead." Poppy explained.

The collapse on the floor was making more sense to Russell, "Oh, so very sorry for your loss, how did it happen?"

"Actually, it happened almost nine years ago, but I just found out." Russell would chew on that puzzle while she was away. She did not wait around to explain. Poppy knew she was a challenging girl, but Russell was a bright man who handled his challenges well.

At the cemetery, Poppy wished she had thought to bring flowers for Lilac's grave…next time, when she had more time to stop there. Her mother would understand and hopefully guide her on this search and find mission. She wondered if the residents here ever communicated among themselves.

Poppy wandered up and down the rows of graves trying not to step directly on them. It would be so much easier if they were arranged in alphabetical order. There were the most basic flat name plates like Lilac's marker, intermingled with tall ornate headstones and even a few monuments. The way a person was immortalized by their headstone, did not equate to the lives they lived, she determined. Her mother's marker was not grand, but Lilac Paisley was well remembered.

Poppy finally found what she was looking for. The newer-appearing headstone was not ostentatious, but tasteful, quite nice really, a remembrance carved in three feet of granite for her old friend and surrogate father. Jaxon had paid appropriate honor to his father. Poppy sat down next to the slab of stone that memorialized Chester J. Cohen and began speaking to him, like she often did at Lilac's graveside.

"Chet are you really buried here? Please help me understand. Why can't I see you now? I need to more than ever. I don't feel as if I'm insane." Poppy received the answer she was expecting. None.

After processing her new reality for several minutes at the graveside, Poppy was drawn back to their favorite bench meeting spot, the place where she had last seen the living version of Chet. The path there passed by her semi-hidden car. If a person was not looking for it, they would walk right past without noticing. Poppy considered a backseat nap when she spied Sunny-mobile but was too wound up and exhausted to sleep.

It was a calm morning in the park, no trace of the previous night's violent events remained. She just sat. The bench brought neither Chet, nor Bernie, nor even Obi-Wan to enlighten her. Poppy was not sure what she was expecting, but definitely not who did come. She was more surprised to see Xavier Max, than if a dead person had sat down next to her.

Xavier plopped solidly onto the metal slats. She felt the shift in weight, but her end of the bench did not rise up like in the cartoons. Xavier Max was definitely a physical being.

"I called the library and Russell told me that I might find you here," in answer to the surprise on Poppy's face. She should never play poker. When Xavier received no answer he continued, "I decided it was time to venture out, to gather writing material and mainly because I keep thinking about the butterfly room."

The change of focus jolted Poppy's vocal chords. "You are off the hook. Jaxon Cohen of Cohen Construction plans to build a library annex, combined with a homeless short-stay shelter here in the park. After I spoke with you, I had the idea to bring the two services together with a butterfly themed connection in the middle. I think the butterflies will end up in this park too. Why not throw them into the bedlam mix that is going on."

Xavier was not sure what bedlam Poppy was alluding to, but answered, "That sounds like an optimal spot for the collection, open it up to the public, so more can share in the beauty and symbolism. Perhaps I can offer funding for the project and be the main sponsor of the new butterfly room?"

"I am sure that would be greatly appreciated." Poppy answered with less than her usual enthusiasm. "You are a man of many surprises Xavier Max. I have to say, I am pretty impressed you ventured out today."

"Yes, I have got to get this hulk moving. However, don't be too impressed. I took an Uber here." Xavier smiled. "Baby steps."

The odd couple sat and exchanged small talk. Poppy watching out of the corner of her eye for the other acquaintance she was waiting for. Suddenly Poppy upped the conversation, "Xavier, have you ever seen something you knew was not really there?"

"You will have to be more specific I am afraid. What are we talking about? Like dreaming you have a hot fudge sundae in the middle of the night?" Xavier asked.

"No, like a person. Someone you knew couldn't actually be there, but they were." Poppy clarified.

Not wanting to offend his new friend with a "heck no" answer, Xavier pondered, "Let me think…one time I didn't *see* a person, but I heard a voice that was not possible."

"What happened?" asked Poppy.

"It was during one of the lowest times of my life. I've had a few of those. I was struggling to even get out of bed. I heard my mother's voice. She had been gone for a few years, not just moved to another house, moved on to another dimension. I had decided to just spend the rest of my obese days in bed. I felt like no one would miss me. Then here comes my spunky mother. She was a tad on the rolly-side herself. No question it was her." Xavier shared.

"Why do you think? What did she say?" Now Poppy was interested.

"It was mainly a kick-in-the-behind pep talk. I am not sure if I can recall the exact words. You would think I would, wouldn't you? She basically told me to hoist my keister out of bed. She reminded me that she believed in me and did not want me wasting my life away. That was pretty much the essence of it. But I decided if she came from the other side to deliver the message, it must be important."

"But why?" Poppy needed to know.

"I determined the Man Upstairs, or someone up there, must care enough to give my mum a pass. When we are barely hanging on by our fingertips, someone must be sent or allowed our way, to help us carry the load for a piece of the journey or motivate us to do so." Xavier reasoned.

"Has she been back? Your mother?" Poppy asked.

"I have not heard her voice, but at times I see other little tokens that remind me she is near and cares about me. Odd things in odder places that only she and I had references to. Is that the kind of thing you are asking about?" Xavier wondered.

"Sort of. That helps. Thanks." Poppy expressed. Maybe Chet was allowed to help her adjust to homelessness and not get frozen. But why not her mom or dad?

By the time Xavier departed, her missing friends had still not made an appearance. Poppy waited a little longer, to make sure the massive man's presence had not prevented their arrival or kept them in hiding. No use. Chet, Bernie and Obi-Wan Kenobi were gone.

"I am not ready to say good-bye." Poppy continued talking, this time to Chet and company, even though they weren't there. "I miss you. I will always be grateful for the time we spent together, and you are welcome back anytime...in body or just voice." It was past time for Poppy to get back to work. She found what she had come to find, just not what or who she had hoped to.

CHAPTER 17

Around 44% of homeless people are employed. The poverty line for a family of four is $24,300. A worker needs to earn $11.70/hour to reach the poverty level for a family of four. A renter needs to earn $21.21/hour to afford a two-bedroom rental in the United States. In only 12 counties in the U.S. can a worker making the federal minimum wage afford a fair-market-rent one-bedroom apartment.

The recent events of the universe seemed to be conspiring against Poppy, keeping her from visits with her grandmother. Their precious time together was slipping through her fingers. As soon as work was over, she booked her way to Greener Pastures.

Director Metcalfe greeted Poppy as she arrived and let her know G-ma Daisy had dropped another step lower on the ladder rungs of health. Poppy could not picture her grandma on a ladder, but she knew what the director was expressing with his metaphor. He continued that Daisy had not communicated with any of the staff for forty-eight hours, which was not a good sign. Her vital signs were deteriorating as well. He suggested Poppy consider staying over tonight and that she may want to spend as much time as she was able in their facility during the next few days. He did not think her grandmother had much time left.

The information was not anywhere close to what Poppy hoped to hear. There was enough drama going on in her circle of friends. She needed a stable family place. "Grandma, you cannot leave me too." Poppy whispered as she headed down the hall to the place she had labeled her legal homeroom. "Don't go yet. Please."

Daisy's head was facing upward, resting comfortably on the pillow, when Poppy entered. Grandma did not stir. Her purple eyelids with virtually no lashes left were shut. Her breathing was slow and deep, but not terribly labored. Maybe Dr. Metcalfe was mistaken, either way Poppy would definitely stay the night, she had hoped to anyway.

The room was quiet and still. There was a peaceful feeling, not at all like death was near, but Poppy was not sure what dying should feel like. It was not tranquil in her mother's case, but nothing about Lilac was. Poppy did not turn on the television or pull out a book to read, she just wanted to soak up every essence of her grandmother. "I am so sorry I have not been here for you more lately grandmother. Things have been pretty crazy, even difficult. I was not abandoning you."

Her grandmother had not been a go-to-church-every-Sunday believer, but she read the Bible daily and she lived what she read. Daisy often shared passages that had meaning to her with Poppy. Poppy slid open the drawer in the bedside stand and lifted out a Gideon Bible that rested there. Thumbing through the pages she came to Psalms and recognized words G-ma Daisy had read to her. They seemed especially applicable at the moment. Poppy read aloud Psalms 23 verse 4...*Yea, though I walk through the valley of the shadow of death, I will fear no evil: for thou art with me; thy rod and thy staff they comfort me....* She hoped her grandma was currently comforted.

Poppy sighed, she leaned back and rehearsed aloud the events of the last few days. They sounded even more bizarre verbalized, more likely to be found in one of the books she would check out of the library. With the telling of all that had happened, some of the weight from current events lifted from Poppy's shoulders. After the saga was all poured out, Poppy laid her head on G-ma Daisy's shoulder. She matched her breathing with the breaths taken in and blown out by the semi-conscious older woman, her cherished mentor. The simple connection was soothing and satisfying to Poppy's soul. Poppy did not sleep. They were communicating heart to heart, breath by breath. It was enough.

There was a soft knock at the door and it opened to Mona, standing there in the flesh.

"You know you are not welcome here. It looks like my grandmother will be going where you wanted to send her without any of your help." Poppy snapped.

"Just give me three minutes to clear the air and I will leave you two to your gentle good-byes," Mona requested.

"I saw what I saw and heard what I heard." Poppy said flatly.

"And what exactly was that?" Mona asked.

"Well, there was you telling Miss Whitley that you would help her see Gerald that night. We both know where Gerald is," Poppy challenged.

"And is Miss Whitley still here?" Mona questioned.

"Yes, but I told Director Metcalfe about your plan. He stopped you." Poppy told her.

"Things are not always what they seem. I was taking Miss Whitley her sleeping pill that night. She had been very agitated, and it helps her get some sleep. She hates pills, but when she does finally get some sleep, she dreams of her lost beloved. She will share some of those dreams with me the following mornings and seems so happy. I was just trying to comfort her and let her know that if she took the tablet, she could go see Gerald…in her dreams." Mona explained.

Poppy was very aware that things were not always what they seemed, but she was not convinced. "What about offering to help me 'take things into my own hands' and 'things don't have to be ugly at the end'?" Poppy challenged.

"I can see that does sound incriminating. What I should have said, is that I have naturopathic remedies and medicines that Green Pastures as a medical unit does not offer. I did not want Mrs. Butterfield to suffer and had other options available for her. Only offered if you did not think the medical cocktails she received here were keeping her comfortable. I should not have interfered, but I truly had no intention to end her life." Mona shared.

Poppy was not sure what to believe. This could be a logical explanation, or the angel of death could just be good at covering her tracks. Tonight, she did not want to worry about it, in her grandmother's current condition, it was now a moot point. "Thank you for the little heart to heart chat, Ms. Mona. However, we will no longer need your services either way." Poppy dismissed the clandestine homeopathic

CNA. She turned back to G-ma Daisy, still sleeping soundly.

There was another rap at the door. "I think we are done." Poppy called out, thinking it was Mona.

Another much younger care giver entered the room. "Done with what? Is Ms. Daisy gone? I have just been looking for better lip balm. I brought some if you would like to try it?" The confused girl offered.

"Sorry. I thought you were someone else. G-ma Daisy is still here. What about a better lip balm?" Poppy was confused too.

"I just want Mrs. Butterfield to be comfortable. The only words she has spoken my whole shift, and the last one too, are about her lips. She is not really awake or conscious, but she will mumble in her sleep about her 'two lips' or something about her lip. She is a little hard to understand clearly. I thought her lips may be bothering her. I gave her some ice chips in case her mouth was dry and have located some better ointment." The young CNA, name-tagged Brinley, handed Poppy the tube of gel.

"Thank you." Poppy took the medicated cream from Brinley. Her grandmother's lips looked fine to her, but just in case she needed it. "She has been pretty quiet, just sleeping, since I've been here."

Brinley checked G-ma Daisy's pulse and blood pressure. "I will give you some time alone, but if you need anything at all please don't hesitate to call me." The nurse pointed to the call button at the head of the bed. "Her vital signs are steady right now." Then she exited the room.

Daisy Butterfield roused as the door closed but did not totally wake. She settled back on the pillow for a few moments, then suddenly sat upright. "Two lip. Two lip." She uttered before lying back down.

Poppy reached for the lip balm Brinley had left her. She unscrewed the cap and squeezed a smidgen onto her finger before the impact of her grandmother's words registered. G-ma Daisy was not requesting something for her two lips. She was calling her dear departed sister, Tulip. Tulip who had passed away years before Poppy was born, but whom she had heard all about. Tulip who had been Daisy's identical sidekick until she died prematurely in her late teens. Was her grandma requesting her sister, or was her sister already here?

Poppy visually checked out all the corners of the room carefully. She did not notice anything unusual. There was no shimmer of light or flutter of a curtain. After her experience with Chester and Bernie, she was almost surprised she could not see her departed great aunt clearly, if she was currently in the room with them. Poppy wondered if she had acquired some x-ray, or gamma-ray, or supernatural-ray vision of some kind, there must have been some factor to enable her to see her homeless friends. What other explanation was there? Unless…there was the schizophrenia possibility too; hopefully not. Maybe her grandma was just having a good dream, like Delta Dawn did of Gerald, because Poppy saw no one.

Poppy had declined the cot to sleep on. She wanted to sit by her grandma's beside; she did not want to fall into such a deep sleep that she missed anything. However, the jet-lag-like emotional crash from her last few days of excitement was catching up with her. Poppy dosed off and on with her head near G-ma Daisy's on the edge of the pillow, while her bottom was planted firmly in the bedside chair. The deep breathing coming from Daisy became more intermittent, with her mouth open and with occasional bursts of loud snores. The night light cast a silhouette of two heads on the twin bed. One with a sparse, thinning gray bun, the other with thick auburn waves tossed between the grandmother and granddaughter on the pillow. It was a touching snapshot, from heaven's view.

The night wore on. Around four o'clock A.M. Grandma Daisy suddenly woke Poppy from a deep dose.

"Tulip is here. She has come to get me." Daisy seemed super excited about whatever was happening.

Poppy was wide awake. "Grandma do you see Tulip?"

"Yes, she's here, and my Grandma Dahlia is with her. I think I see Henry hanging in the background too." Although feeble, Daisy sounded alert and more like herself than she had in two years. There was a strength and clarity about her grandmother that caused Poppy to be totally present for whatever she was about to receive.

"Is my mom Lilac here?" Poppy was curious.

"No, those are the only ones I can see. But they all look so beautiful and handsome." Daisy said with emotion. Poppy imaged her mother was probably off painting flowers in some corner of heaven. Lilac was not one for social gatherings.

"Tell me what you can see?" Poppy could still not see a thing, but she could compare it to her recent viewing of deceased beings.

"Tulip looks just like she did before she died. She was always the prettier twin, but now she is glorious. She wants me to go with her. Grandma Dahlia came to accompany her on the journey. They are not talking with their mouths, but I can hear them communicate in my mind.

Grandma doesn't look much older than Tulip, but she still has the same sparkle I remember in her golden-brown eyes. It is her. Tulip and I were always her favorites. I sense Henry is worried what I will think about him and wants Tulip to have her time with me first. He looks like he did when we were married. That man always did take my breath away. Oh Poppy, I am so happy to see them. I wish you could see them too." Daisy said.

There was an energy in the room that was undeniable. Poppy did not doubt that what her grandmother was telling her was true. Especially after having spent time recently with other people who had previously been buried. But if they had come to get G-ma Daisy, why did her grandmother seem so much healthier and more alive than she did minutes ago.

"Poppy, I think I need to go with them. Will you be okay my darling girl? I hate to leave you." Daisy's eyes filled with tears, but there was joy and a youthfulness spreading across her aged face.

"Grandma, I will miss you more than you know. You have been everything a little girl could dream of, but I want you to be happy. It seems like it may be your time to go..." Poppy wanted to beg her to stay but knew it would only be for selfish reasons. "I will be okay. You have taught me well." Poppy doubted she could keep the cherished woman here, even if she had wanted to. "Of course, you can go."

G-ma Daisy's body was still lying peacefully on the bed, but immediately Poppy sensed that part of her grandma was gone. The best part of her. In reality, much of that part had been missing for some time. Poppy heard one loud gurgling breath and then silence. There was a tangible feeling of immense love radiating from around the bed, but her grandma, her cute, fun, source of comfort and belonging, G-ma Daisy, was no longer living. At least her body was not. Poppy dropped her head into her hands, tears rolled between her fingers and rained onto the bed's blankets.

Now she really was alone. Poppy would not even have an official address to call home. She almost wished her grandmother had taken her along with her, when she passed on to the other side.

CHAPTER 18

Cities are increasingly making homelessness a crime. A 2014 survey of 187 cities by the NLCHP found that 24 percent of cities make it a city-wide crime to beg in public, 33 percent make it illegal to stand around or loiter anyplace in the city, 18 percent make it a crime to sleep anywhere in public, 43 percent make it illegal to sleep in your car, and 53 percent make it illegal to sit or lie down in particular public places. And the number of cities criminalizing homelessness is steadily increasing. In some places, like Hawaii, officials have attempted to solve homelessness by providing one-way plane tickets elsewhere.

The first fingers of morning light were beginning to touch the sky before Poppy pushed the call button. The clock showed shortly after six A.M. She savored those last moments alone before the staff began all their medical processing and took her grandmother's beloved, but quickly cooling body away. Although Poppy had known Daisy's demise was imminent, the end came too fast. There is never enough time.

Around seven o'clock, Dr. Metcalfe entered the room of the recently deceased with an air of reverence. "My condolences Miss Paisley, Mrs. Butterfield was a delightful woman. I am here to assist you with whatever you need at this difficult time. Your grandmother's care package with us included a small burial benefit which allows basic mortuary care of the body and a graveside service."

The director's comments made things all too real. "That will be enough. Most of her friends and family are already gone." Poppy responded. "She was a simple woman who would not have wanted anything fancy."

"We have already sent word to Larkin Mortuary. They should arrive soon. Can I do anything else for you?" Director Metcalfe asked.

Could he do anything else for her? Where should she begin? But Poppy just answered, "Thank you for giving my grandmother a safe home during her last few years and for everything else you are already doing to help with her interment. I will be fine." I always am, she thought.

Poppy did not want to watch her grandmother being prepped and taken away. She wandered down the hall to Greener Pastures' tiny chapel and sat on a pew beneath a small stained-glass window. Nowhere was now home with

Grandma gone. Where would she go? Where would she live? Poppy would now have the finances she needed to find a place of her own, separate from the care center. She just had to figure out where she belonged. She would much rather have her grandma here and still reside in Sunny-mobile.

The irony of having wished so hard for a home hit her. A house itself is not necessarily a domicile of safety. Just because a person has shelter over their head, did not make it a home like one she dreamed of. Xavier's impressive home was a huge, tantalizing food cave for him much of the time. Russell's home appeared to be an isolation chamber where he pined for company. Butterfly girl Aporia's home had literally been her prison. Grandma Daisy's last home may have been a euthanasia friendly facility. Perhaps her grandmother's home didn't have walls at all but was the place she was trapped in her own mind. Chet and Bernie's home became their frozen tomb.

Poppy realized she had had a home, just not a house to put it in. Home was merely a place each person created, where they felt belonging and hopefully peace. Physical walls were optional. Where in the world was that place for Poppy now?

With few preparations needed, the basic service to honor Daisy Butterfield's life was held two days later. A few former friends and neighbors from their Tooterville neighborhood showed up. Poppy wondered how they had even heard. Bad news travels much faster than good news she supposed.

Moriah had stayed at the library to keep things running but let Russell attend. It had not been easy for him to roll the wheels of his chair across the grassy terrain to the pre-dug hole in the ground that would be her grandmother's final resting place. Her friend had spiffed himself up. Russell was wearing a dress shirt with black tie. His blondish hair was combed back more formally than his everyday style. It was comforting to see her solid support system sitting there.

Xavier Max showed up too. He was becoming a dang social butterfly, odd choice of metaphors in her world. His wide girth could not be contained by the width of the standard folding chair and lopped over its sides. The large man looked uncomfortable but determined. Poppy was touched at his efforts to support her in her time of grief, over his own discomfort.

Jaxon Cohen appeared in his overcoat and dress hat. He stood awkwardly at the back of the small group. The look in his eyes conveyed his sorrow for her loss. Poppy needed to let him know that she was sorry as well. He had told the truth. His father was indeed buried not far from this plot where they now gathered. Her self-righteous attitude about parent and grandparent care had been amiss.

The three men, who all cared for her in their own way, were each so very different. Not only polar opposites, but triangular opposites. If Chet had shown up, the analogy could be enlarged to quadrangular opposites. Where were Chet and Bernie? Chet's resting place was close enough it would not take him much effort to float by for the thirty minutes.

Misty was still incarcerated at the psych hospital and Poppy doubted she would have come to pay her respects anyway, under their parting circumstances. She supposed Aporia was settled in her foster home. A funeral was not exactly the place to get re-acclimated to normal life. Poppy mentally committed to pay the poor girl a visit at her first opportunity, after this chapter of her life had closed.

The mortuary's minister opened his Bible and shared a passage from Ecclesiastes:

To everything there is a season, and a time to every purpose under the heaven;

A time to be born, and a time to die; a time to plant, and a time to pluck up that which is planted;

A time to kill, and a time to heal; a time to break down, and a time to build up;

A time to weep, and a time to laugh; a time to mourn, and a time to dance;

A time to cast away stones, and a time to gather stones together; a time to embrace, and a time to refrain from embracing;

A time to get, and a time to lose; a time to keep, and a time to cast away;

A time to rend, and a time to sew; a time to keep silence, and a time to speak;

A time to love, and a time to hate; a time of war, and a time of peace.

Next on the program, those in attendance were supposed to sing the song *Come Thou Font of Every Blessing.* Poppy was moved by the melodious melody and lyrics, but none of those present really knew the selected song well enough to give the words on the printed page their due justice. Larkin Mortuary's representative virtually sang a solo in his clear tenor voice, while the rest of them joined in for a word or phrase here and there. The effect was still sweet. Poppy's heart felt a tenderness for those who had come and especially the guest of honor in the simply-elegant pine casket before her.

The gentleman conducting the affair asked if anyone wanted to step forward to say a few words over Daisy Butterfield's grave. There was silence. None of Poppy's friends knew her grandmother and the few who were there from the old neighborhood were not personalities who would be at home in front of even the small crowd.

Poppy rose to stand beside the unadorned casket. She would not let it be lowered into the earth without a proper send off. "I wish all of you had known my Grandma Daisy like I did. She was a beautiful woman inside and out. There was not a selfish bone in her body. Any girl would have been lucky to have been raised by this spunky lady. She taught me to see the beauty in every day and to be kind to every person whose path I crossed. Whenever I was having a bad day, she would find a way to turn it around. Usually by having us do something for someone less fortunate than ourselves. I have tears in my eyes today, but I laughed much more than I cried when I was around my grandmother. The world will lose a bright light with her burial. She was one of the best flowers in the bouquet. I will miss her more than I can say..." Poppy felt a lump of emotion welling up in her throat and did not know what else to add.

She slid a single daisy from the large bouquet, the rest she intended to lay across the fresh dirt mound after the box containing her grandma had been covered. The bereft granddaughter gently placed the namesake flower on the coffin's lid before it dropped into the ground.

Cremation would have been cheaper, but it didn't feel right to Poppy. Daisy had purchased a second plot when she acquired one for Lilac fourteen years ago. There had been a deal on double plots, like a two-for-one special. Daisy Butterfield had not known at the time it would be her final resting place. Poppy had to make that choice. Her flower grandma Daisy would be planted next to her flower mother Lilac. Flowers needed to put into the soil and not burned to ashes. It would also make Poppy's visits to them both so convenient.

Each person filed by and dropped a handful of dirt into the hole. Then stood back waiting to see what would be required of them next. Poppy just wanted them all to fade away and let her sit and pay her last respects in solitude. First, she must make the rounds to thank each person for their attendance and the part they played in her grandmother's life as well as her own. She saved her three gentlemen friends for last.

They all knew each other, or of each other, but Poppy preferred private conversations to a group discussion. She walked up to Xavier Max first. He rose from the folding chair that had held up under his weigh throughout the services. Poppy gave Xavier a hug, wrapping her arms around his thick neck, trying to fit them around his waist would have been awkward for them both. With sincerity she thanked the man for coming and for all he was willing to do for her at a minute's notice. She was impressed he was here, out and about just a few days since she had last visited with him in this very park. Xavier nonchalantly accepted Poppy's praise and said he looked forward to her next book visit, before he wandered away into the sunset.

Russell would be easier to talk to. They always had more to say to each other, so normally she would save his conversation for last. But Poppy, for some reason, did not want him to be there when she visited with Jaxon Cohen. She did not know what she was going to say to the board member to make things right between them.

Russell came to her, before she got the chance to move his way. "Poppy I am devastated for your loss. Why don't you stay at my apartment tonight? I don't want you to be alone."

"That is such a generous offer Russell. You are too kind. I think I will just sit here for a while with grandma and think things through, but I will let you know." Poppy bent at the waist to wrap Russell in a full torso hug. His waist was pressed tight against the chair and the affection she felt for him required more than a neck hug today. He readily reciprocated stretching his arms around her back. It may not have been a traditional embrace, but what was traditional in Poppy's life? "Thank you for coming today. It means more than you know." Poppy spoke softly into Russell's right ear before he forcefully stroked the top of his wheels and rolled himself away.

The only person left, besides the mortuary man, was her intended apology recipient. Jaxon Cohen had hung back until the others dispersed. "I truly am sorry for your loss Miss Paisley."

"Thank you for coming, I did not expect you to be here. You can call me Poppy." Unless he preferred to keep things formal and businesslike between them. "I think I am the one who owes you an apology. May I ask for your forgiveness?"

Of course, I am just curious why you thought my father was currently living in the park?" Jaxon inquired.

Poppy was not ready for full transparency. She wanted the man to completely forgive her before he decided she was a lunatic. "That will be a story for another day, if you will allow me to wait. Let's just call it a case of mistaken identity for now." She had mistaken a dead man for a living one.

"Still a woman of mystery I see. At least you can make it up to me with a cemetery visit and dinner date next week. We can pay respects to our family members together here, then grab something to eat." Jaxon suggested.

"I think I can make that work." Poppy answered, surprised at how deeply she really desired to.

Jaxon Cohen moved in for the good-bye embrace he had seen her offer the others. Their arms naturally entwined around one another and Jaxon casually dropped his head onto Poppy's shoulder. The act felt oddly intimate. As he released her, Jaxon's lips brushed Poppy's forehead gently, leaving a warm tingle that spread to her scalp. This man had the magic touch.

"Until next week then." Jaxon said as he turned and headed toward Chet's grave. Poppy watched his retreating figure until it disappeared behind some bushes.

As she turned back to continue her solo good-bye, on the knoll to the west she noticed Office Platt watching from the distance. She was not sure if he was overseeing the service in an official capacity or had come to pay his respects. He was one of the good guys. The policeman had left her abandoned car undisturbed where he had discovered her in it last week. That is where Poppy would sleep tonight. She would stay near her grandma, here in Sunny-mobile, until she figured out where her new home was...where she now belonged.

CHAPTER 19

In total, 33 states and the District of Columbia (D.C.) have reported decreases in overall homelessness, while 16 states reported increases in the past few years. The last time a global survey was attempted by the United Nations an estimated 100 million people were homeless worldwide. As many as 1.6 billion people who live on this planet lack adequate housing. (Habitat, 2015).

The next few weeks were foggy for Poppy. She just existed. It was strange to no longer drop in daily at Greener Pastures. She missed her visits there, but most of all, she missed her Grandma Daisy. Her days consisted of work at the library, studying for her classes, looking for a place to live and regular visits to the cemetery.

Poppy's residential needs had been honed and given greater perspective over the last few years of her not-really-homeless living. She checked out a few places she came upon in the classified ads for possible habitats, but none seemed worth the price they were asking for rent. She knew her needs were minimal and could not justify all the unneeded extras.

Poppy finally stumbled upon an attic studio apartment, over a garage, near the park and cemetery. There was a red and white 'for rent' sign posted in the yard when she walked by one day. It was a furnished walk-up, with wooden staircase, between the cemetery and the library, her two top stops. Large windows let in light and the bright colors reminded her of her mother's flower-painted walls. It was the first place that felt like home to her. The fact that it did not have a dishwasher or bathtub did not matter in the least but had discouraged other tenants and had kept the price low. A shower was fine, and Poppy was used to not cooking much, so dishes would be few. She was home.

One weekend after moving in, Regina Bozeman was willing to take Poppy to visit Aporia. Poppy had wanted to go see her again ever since meeting with her in the hospital, but the logistics and loss of her grandmother had stymied her plans. She needed transportation and having someone with her on the first visit was a plus. Sunny-mobile either needed a mechanic's touch or Poppy needed to consider getting a new vehicle, but she was taking her new-life needs one step forward at a time.

On the way over, Regina explained that Aporia wanted to live with her mother again in spite of her abuse, which was not unusual. And the hospital thought that might eventually be a possibility. Misty was doing well on her medications and seemed to be fairly stable. When Aporia was given permission to visit her mother at the mental hospital, before moving in with the foster care family, things had gone better than the medial staff had hoped. The two hesitantly embraced upon seeing each other, tears gleaming in both of their eyes.

Misty apologized repeatedly, gushing out her good intentions that had gone so wrong. Aporia was amazingly forgiving and a victim who refused to prosecute. She was more concerned to know if her mother was indeed going to be okay. So, it seemed just a matter of time until Misty was well enough to be released. A mother might incarcerate her child, but it appeared, if it was with their child's best interest in mind, even if the mother were in a deluded state, she could be given a second chance.

Poppy was happy that Misty was improving, and she hoped a permanent reunion worked out for the mother and daughter duo. She wondered, if Lilac had spent some time in a mental facility, if her own life may have been different, but she did not dwell there long. The things she experienced along her journey had made her the person she was, and Poppy was getting to know and like that girl.

Aporia was timid when Poppy first arrived. The relocated girl looked healthy, but not surprisingly, was quite tentative and emotionally closed. The home she was saying in was a basic suburbia ranch-style home. The foster parents appeared nice and polite. There were two biological children in the home as well. They all exchanged pleasantries and their interchange was respectfully superficial.

When Poppy got comfortable enough to ask, she suggested that maybe she and Aporia could spend a little time alone. When the CSD worker and foster parents agreed, the two motherless daughters ventured into the backyard. They sat down side by side on two matching swings and glided back and forth in the cool air.

"Would you like to know about your grandmother? I met her in the park." Poppy offered. "My grandmother was very special to me, so I thought you might like to know a little about yours."

Aporia quietly answered. "You knew my grandma? I think I would like to hear about her."

Poppy realized she was trending on sacred ground and planned to leave out the fact that her grandma Bernie was actually dead before she knew her. She proceeded to share with Aporia stories of her visits with Bernice. Poppy told of things she knew to be true and introduced Aporia to the tough, yet fun woman Bernie was. She shared that Bernie had a dog and told her all about Obi-Wan Kenobi and how he had been named for a Jedi master in the *Star Wars* movies. She even let Aporia know that even though her mother Misty and grandmother Bernice had argued long ago and separated, that Bernie still loved Misty very much. Bernie may not even have known that Aporia had been born. She regretted her argument with Misty and wished she could have a do-over, so she could have had them both in her life.

The last part Poppy may have extrapolated to historical fiction but knowing Bernie the way she did and meeting Aporia, Poppy was pretty sure what the outcome would have, and should have, been had the two found each other earlier.

Aporia came out of her cocoon and looked like a full-on butterfly. She swung into the air higher and higher on the swing. "Do you think I could meet my grandmother one day?"

The truth always seemed to be the best policy, when a hard topic emerged, "I am sorry Aporia, your Grandma Bernie has passed away. But I want to come and visit with you regularly in her place, so you can get to know the woman I knew. That is the least I can do for both of you. Would that be okay?"

"I would like that. And maybe you can tell my mom about her too when she gets home. I think that would make her happy." Aporia kept swinging. Poppy matched her own rhythm to be in-sync with the fragile young girl. She could see herself on the parallel swing and hoped to be a part of Aporia's life for some time into the future.

Poppy wanted to invite Russell for a 'thank you' dinner, to pay him back a teensy particle of all he had done for her. After pondering several options, she realized there was no way for him get up to her apartment. She had not thought that little detail through when renting the place. She was so used to living alone and never invited over company to entertain at her various temporary residences.

As an alternate, Poppy asked Russell to join her at a local restaurant with home-cooked dining. Her treat. Hughes Cafe was owned by the Hughes family, with the hyphen added for a little twist. It would be her food-hug for Russell. They arranged to meet there after work on Saturday.

Poppy arrived early and asked to be seated at a handicap friendly table where Russell could just roll up and park in his chair. She told Russell to come in casual dress. Poppy wore her straight-legged black slacks with long-sleeved pink pullover. She had taken out her ponytail and her hair cascaded down around her shoulders. Poppy watched out the window for her friend, co-worker, guy-pal… she was not really sure what Russell was to her…to arrive.

Before long, Russell arrived looking handsome in his black crewneck sweater and jeans. His upper body was ultra-fit and developed, due to the constant workout it received daily. His arms were his legs. His slender legs lay still, knees propped up by his feet on the foot rests.

"You look absolutely smashing Poppy girl. So nice of you to invite me out to dinner. However, I am not sure a gentleman would let his date pay." Russell mentioned as her pulled up and slid under the table. "Perfect table with a view. Nice job. For future reference, I can hoist myself out of my chair and slide into a booth if needed." Russell was so comfortable and open with her. Poppy felt a little guilty she had not given him the same credit. Tonight, was time to come clean with true confessions.

"I have recently come into some extra funds and insist on picking up the check. Since I cannot cook for you, this is my small thank you, for you being you in my life." Poppy decided to wait to discuss heavier things over food, the distraction of eating may lessen the impact.

A tall male waiter with a tidy man-bun, took their orders. Poppy ordered a cobb salad with blue cheese dressing and Russell the fish and chips. Over sodas, while waiting for their food, they discussed the library and people that worked there. Poppy wondered what else they had in common. Books for sure, but she asked him about his other interests. Russell was indeed well-rounded, enjoying many activities she had no idea he pursued... music, theater, sports... they had tons to talk about.

Half way through dinner Poppy knew it was time. "I have a confession to make Russell. I should have told you before, but I was too embarrassed." There was a long pause, but Russell waited, letting Poppy take her time to get out what had been so hard for her to share. "I have not really had a permanent place to live for quite a while. I have stayed wherever I could each night, my car, the care center, and that morning you caught me at the library so early, I had been sleeping there." There, it was out.

"It's okay. I have known, for quite a while actually. That is one of the reasons I always extended invitations for you to come study or stay at my place. But I started to worry I was coming on too strong. I didn't want you to think that I wanted something more from you." Russell told her.

"Russell, why didn't you tell me you knew?!" Poppy was shocked.

"I knew you would tell me when you were ready." Russell responded. "And I kept track on my own to make sure you were alright."

Tears pooled in Poppy's eyes. She felt so much emotion for this man. Without thinking, she stood up and leaned across the table planting a full mouth kiss on Russell's surprised, but welcoming, lips.

"If I would have known that was coming, I would have told you much earlier." Russell teased.

The kiss was sweet, although slightly sloppy, and not what either Poppy or Russell would call romantic by any stretch of the imagination. Poppy did care for Russell, in fact she thought she might love him. Russell definitely loved Poppy, but the love he felt for her was complicated.

He needed to define it more before he accepted her tenderized-by-life heart. What did he feel?

There was no doubt Poppy was lovely. Any man with two eyes and reasonably good sense would be attracted to her. Russell loved to flirt with her at work, she had been a conquest he now realized he could win if he chose. He had slayed her dragon and been rewarded the flower princess herself. It gave him a heady feeling to know the guy in the wheelchair could get the cute girl at work, if he wanted. In many ways he would love that. But sitting before him now was a fragile creature, a woman who had just completed one of life's most difficult battles. He did not want to swoop in for the score, unless he was sure it was a forever thing. Poppy's emotions were not to be toyed with. He cared about her far too much. Were his feelings more what one would have as a protective big brother…perhaps she was the little sister he never had? What in the world…was he wonky?

No, Russell knew he did not want to hurt the newly declared recently homeless girl for even a moment. He always wanted to be a supportive part of her life. This may not be the time for him to pursue romance, but to come forth with his new info as well. "I have a confession to tell you tonight too." Russell peaked Poppy's curiosity.

"Xavier invited me to accompany him, 'as a friend and traveling companion, not as a manservant or boyfriend' …those were his exact words, not mine…on a world tour."

"What?!" was all Poppy could get out after her second surprise of the evening.

"You know Xavier, he is an extremist in all things. He wants to make up for lost time being shut in. The trip will be used as a resource for the books he hopes to write. He plans to finance both of our travel, in exchange for my literary insights and companionship. We will be back for the opening of the library annex and homeless shelter with butterfly room. Xavier does not want to miss the unveiling of his latest pet, or should I say winged, project. He would have asked you to go, but felt traveling with a woman would complicate things, with lodging and all. Not that traveling with a man in a wheelchair won't be a bit of a complication as well." Russell updated Poppy on his news.

"Wow Russell. I am so happy for you." And she was for the most part.

"Just say the word Poppy and I will stay. If you need me in any capacity, I will not go." Russell offered. From the bottom of his heart, he had originally hoped she would plead with him to stay and profess that she could not live without him. However, after the impromptu kiss and taking

231

mental evaluation of their relationship, he did not want to lead her on or give her the wrong impression. "Can I just adopt you as my little sister?"

Poppy would miss Russell immensely, but she did not want to hold him back in any way. He had made the boundaries of their relationship clear. She had just been shut down as a serious romantic partner. "Of course, I will miss you so much Russell, but you must go. I would never want you to miss out on such an amazing adventure. Take notes and lots of pictures for me too. You can share them with me when you get back. Then of course you must email me all along the way. I would love to have you as a big brother. I really don't have any family left and you are the only person that comes anywhere close to fitting that category in my life." Poppy was willing to keep Russell in her life in whatever kind of relationship he would allow.

"You couldn't get rid of me if you tried I'm afraid." He responded. Perhaps his feelings for Poppy would morph and grow into something different with time and distance. He had heard absence makes the heart grow fonder. But for now, this felt right, he had to be sure.

They finished their meals and shared a warm marionberry cobbler a la mode before calling it a night. For the first time, Poppy finally admitted to herself as well as to Russell, she really had been homeless.

CHAPTER 20

Homeless families are often hidden from our view, living in shelters, cars, campgrounds, or doubled up in overcrowded apartments. About 0.5 percent of the U.S. population has used an emergency shelter or a transitional housing program. The effects of homelessness on homeless people are large. They range from health issues to personal entrapment. It is believed that many homeless individuals failed in their lives to cope with their difficulties and this makes them alienate themselves from the rest of the world. A study at Princeton found that our brains tend to process images of homeless people more like they process objects than actual human beings.

Jaxon Cohen called the library a few days later to follow up on his cemetery dinner-date proposal. Poppy was excited to go out with her favorite library board member but requested that she be allowed to plan a picnic in the park for him instead. She still had a few items to resolve.

At first Jaxon argued that it may be too cold, but Poppy convinced him. She pointed out that the park was the perfect place to discuss and honor those who ate and lived there daily. They could gain perspective for his project as they chewed. He still preferred fine dining with an elegant atmosphere and linen cloths, but acquiesced.

Poppy gathered some fun picnic foods for the occasion. She built turkey, bacon and avocado sandwiches topped with lettuce and tomatoes on thick-sliced wheat bread. Beside the sandwiches, she packed a bunch of green grapes, baby carrots and cucumber slices with dill dip and homemade chocolate chip cookies for dessert. Cookies were less messy to eat outdoors than her deliciously moist chocolate cake would be. Her cache of impressive recipes was very limited, so she'd save the cake for another special occasion.

To help cut through the cold, she added a thermos of hot cocoa to the basket. Then, on top of the edible items, she threw in all of the paper products they would need, along with a warm blanket. It was not a feast fit for a king, or even a construction mogul, but much better than any meal most of those who ate in the park would ever get. She decided to also fill a few lunch sacks with extra food, in case any hungry-looking park dwellers came upon their picnic. They would share.

The two met at the cemetery. They paid respects at their loved ones' graves first, then walked by the spot for the future library annex and shelter, before settling down on the infamous park bench to consume their food. Jaxon was generous with his compliments of the casual picnic basket fare. With the project site in close vicinity, it was foremost on their brains and a natural topic of conversation.

"You should know, the library project has been fully approved, not only by the entire library board, but by the city council as well. We plan to break ground next month when the weather is more reliable. The college is tending to the butterflies in their science department until we are ready for them. They were thrilled to take a turn." Jaxon opened.

"That is such outstanding news. I guess this can be a celebratory meal as well. I wonder if Misty will want at least some of the butterflies back one day. I guess we can cross that bridge when we come to it." Poppy commented. "They may hold bad memories for her and especially for Aporia now."

"We could name the building after them or do something to incorporate the butterfly theme. I don't want it named after my father, although he may seem the logical choice. He was a great man and my main source of inspiration for the project, but we share the same name as you know. I don't feel worthy of, nor would I be comfortable with, the honor." Jaxon shared.

"You sell yourself short C. J. Cohen Jr. You are a good man too. I know your father would be proud." Poppy said.

"How can you know that? You didn't know my father." Jaxon answered solemnly.

"We can discuss that more later. I have another idea. How about literally designing the building in the shape of a butterfly. Have one huge wing be for the library annex, the other wing can house the shelter component and the butterfly room in the middle can be its body. Naming it after a butterfly might be misleading and may not attract the intended clientele. Let the shape represent our intent. We are hoping to assist them out of their homeless cocoons and encourage them to become the butterflies they can be. Building a huge butterfly building and using the butterfly as a symbol, should be more than enough." Poppy threw her random idea out there.

"A very creative vision, Poppy Paisley. I will touch base with the architects and get their input." Jaxon replied. "Any ideas on a name?"

"Maybe use a play on words and call it merely *The Inn*? You know, a place where no one is turned away, unlike Christ's day. Or find a name that lets people know it will be a place to nurture the body and the mind, with both beds and books available." Poppy suggested.

"Like *Bed & Book* instead of Bed & Breakfast?" Jaxon asked.

"That could be cool. Use the butterfly symbol with *Bed* written on one wing, the *&* sign on the body, and *Book* on the other wing." Poppy chuckled.

"I can picture it now." Jaxon mused. "Marketing may not be the first area we need to focus on, but I can definitely see the image as a possible logo to shoot for." They finished off the turkey sandwiches and were munching on the veggies and grapes.

Feeling suddenly nervous, Poppy decided to stall her confessions slightly longer, "Tell me a little about yourself, Mr. C. J. Cohen, besides what I already know...that you are easy on the eyes, compassionate, and a library board member who owns a constructions company."

"Not sure what you would like to know. My life is not really too exciting. I grew here in St. Anthony. I have an older sister, Carly. She got married will I was still pretty young and moved to Utah with her husband. She wasn't interested in resurrecting the family business. Her husband is a doctor and they have four kids. I only see them every

239

other year or so. After my father left, and then passed away shortly after, my mother struggled. She decided to move closer to the grandkids. Mom comes to visit me, and dad, at least once a year and sometimes we take a trip together." Jason shared.

"Any unusual interests or hobbies?" Poppy continued.

"Not very unusual, I would think. I keep busy working long hours with my business. I play a round of golf now and then. I enjoy books as you must have deduced from the library board gig. I follow a few sports teams and on especially boring weekends used to binge watch Netflix. Helping the homeless is my new and improved pet passion. Is there anything in particular you want to know?" Jaxon seemed unsure what else to share.

"I guess that's good for now. But there are a few non-business-related items that I need to discuss with you, Jaxon." Poppy finally gathered up the courage to blurt out as she served dessert. "The first one is more a confession of sorts."

"I am definitely not a priest, but you may unburden yourself my child, if you would like." Jaxon smiled.

With a deep breath, Poppy dove in. "I know my behavior could be considered slightly strange or even erratic in the past. I haven't been totally forthcoming with you…I was trying to hide the fact I did not really have a place to live. My vested interest in your idea was because I was experiencing the homeless plight firsthand."

Jaxon was slow and thoughtful with his answer. "I am so very sorry and must admit totally astonished. How unaware am I? I had absolutely no idea. The mystery girl's mystery is solved. I know I'm a little late to the party, but how can I help you, after the fact?"

"All's good now. And I was really fine before, I just had to be a bit more creative with the resources around me. Can you understand? My grandmother's care came first." Poppy admitted.

"You truly are an amazing woman. It makes more sense to me now, why you were so hard on me about my father being homeless. Please know, I would have given anything to have been able to provide him with safe shelter and prevent the tragedy that took place. It is awful to lose a parent or grandparent, as you well know." Jaxon responded. "But I still don't have a clue as to why you called me so upset late that night and thought my father was alive."

"I wasn't using any mind-altering substance, in case you think that is the other part of my confession. This next

241

part is going to be substantially more difficult to explain. You may want to withhold your judgements of me until I finish." Poppy said. "I was friends with your father here in the park. I spent time with him and a woman named Bernie and their dog, or a dog I thought was theirs."

"You mean before he died? You would have been quite young." Jaxon recognized.

"No, I know this sounds impossible and insane. But I hung out with them on several occasions over the last two years during my homeless period. They shared their camp with me some nights." Poppy inwardly cringed as she told Jaxon.

"You are right, that not only sounds impossible, it is. You must have been mistaken. Or there was someone impersonating my father." Jaxon sounded stressed and the pitch of his voice rose.

"I have already explored both of those options. But I saw with my own eyes the picture of your father at the board party. I am pretty positive it was him. I got to know the man. He told me all about you and wanted me to meet you. I don't believe the man I knew was a fraud. He was so warm and wise. What did he have to gain by befriending a young homeless woman?" Poppy felt rattled as she intensely shared her observations.

"Let's look at this logically. What you are implying is not feasible. The man, you say you know, has been buried in the ground for nearly nine years." Jaxon reminded her. "Is this a scam of some sort?"

Poppy was horrified that Jaxon could believe that of her and scrambled. "I know it makes no logical sense, that is why I didn't want to tell you. But I decided it was important to give you full disclosure. If I want our friendship or relationship to go anywhere, I have to be real. I can see I overshot the situation and connection."

Jaxon was obviously confused and did not know where to go with the information he had just heard. He looked like he was going to choke on his chocolate chip cookie and thought Poppy may need heavy medication. "You have been through a lot lately Poppy. More than most people could bear. Perhaps you should talk to someone. I am trying not to be skeptical here..."

There it was, he did think she was psycho. Tears began to fill her eyes, Poppy was so frustrated. She guessed it was better to know now, than to start something and find out later she was wrong. She started to tell Jaxon that it was probably time she headed home, when a familiar couple with their dog appeared not very far from where the picnickers sat.

"Son, how could you not believe my lovely Lily?" There was Chet, always coming to Poppy's rescue.

Jaxon looked like he might swallow his tongue. "This cannot be and that is not even her name."

"Mortal minds cannot always wrap themselves around concepts of eternity. Not all things are what they appear. And Poppy has always been a full bouquet of flowers to me." Poppy was ecstatic to see her father-like friend. His timing was impeccable. She had an impulse to hug him but was not even sure there would be anything to hug.

"How? Why?" Both she and Jaxon asked at the same time, looking incredulously at the trio.

"Yes, Bernie and I, with Obi-Wan here, did die in the park that night. Our bodies are buried. Well, mine buried and Bernice was cremated. But neither of us were ready to move on. We both had unfinished business to attend to and were allotted time to wrap up some loose ends." Chet explained.

Poppy wondered if Jaxon might need CPR, but his countenance was beginning to soften slightly. "What did you need to do, dad?"

"I hated to leave you son, until you had someone in your life to help you find happiness again. Then when I met

Poppy, it was natural to do double duty. You both needed me and each other."

Now Jaxon's eyes were moist, "I am seeing and hearing all this, but it is still hard to believe."

"I understand the quandary. It makes a person ponder how each of us interprets reality doesn't it?" Chet lovingly responded.

Bernie saw an opening in the philosophical discussion and took a turn. "And Poppy figured out my secret I see. I could not abandon my daughter and granddaughter after I saw the dang mess I had created. It was too late to fix the situation myself, so thank you Poppy for intervening in their behalf for me and going in for the rescue. Hopefully they will both heal. Can you tell them I am so, so sorry and have wished a million times I had handled things differently?"

"Who is she?" Jaxon asked totally befuddled.

"Meet Misty's mother and Aporia's grandmother, Bernice Abernathy. I have been telling Aporia about you on my visits Bernie and will share what I know with Misty when I can." Poppy promised. "In return, perhaps you two can say hello to my Grandma Daisy for me, when you eventually get where you are going. She passed while you were away."

"I am sure we will be grand friends with your grandmother." Chet comforted. "I look forward to meeting your whole extended flower chain in the near future."

"You aren't sticking around to see the building go up?" Jaxon asked. "I just found out you were here."

"It feels like our transition is imminent now. Sorry son. I am getting the definite impression we have done all we needed to do in this world and at least my time here is numbered. A flood of peace has overcome me. You will be fine Jaxon. I am so proud of you. Your project here in the park is the legacy I never left you. Thank you. Perhaps I can return for its opening." It felt like Chet was saying goodbye.

Obi-Wan Kenobi came over and licked the palm of Poppy's hand. Perhaps he smelled the food or maybe he was expressing his farewells too. The experience was not like a normal dog's tongue, sandpapery, warm and wet, but there was definitely a tingly tactile connection. Warmth spread across her hand.

"I am not ready to say goodbye yet either. I have lost too many I love. Could you please stick around for a while?" Poppy pleaded.

"You may not see us anymore, but we will be closer than you know. I could never abandon my dear Posy. Your openness and acceptance have made sojourning in this park pure pleasure. We were just carrying on St. Anthony's mission... *to seek lost items or people.* I think you have both been found. Jaxon take care of this girl. She is a special one." Chet was turning over reigns he did not really hold, but it touched Poppy's heart to be cared for.

"I feel like I have missed out on so much. You will be gone again, and I barely knew you were here. Thank you for at least giving me a glimpse." Jaxon was still reeling but trying to absorb the moment. "I will do all I can to honor the name you left me."

It felt like a group hug was in order, but in reality, probably not possible. Instead a warm encompassing cloud of goodwill dropped over the five and a tangible feeling of what must be pure love infused into them all. As the emotion began to dissipate, so did the density of the three deceased presences. Their essences went from opaque, to translucent and then evaporated away.

Poppy and Jaxon sat in silence for many moments, fearful that if they spoke, the magic of the moment would dissolve too. Words were not needed. With love still swirling in the air, Poppy reached over and gave Jaxon Cohen the physical embrace she desired to give the group. She hoped it would help hold onto the tenderness she did not want to lose. The act may not have been as ethereal an experience as the touch-less cuddle, but it evoked another response from its recipient.

Jaxon Cohen, with what felt like all the pent-up emotions of his last nine years, took Poppy Paisley reciprocally in his arms and released such a passionate kiss on her lips, she felt like he might consume her whole. His hungry mouth inhaled her top lip and then moved to her lower lip, before meeting both of her kissable, full, soft, two lips straight on, flesh to flesh with his own.

Jaxon pulled back for breath and huskily spoke, "I apologize, I'm not sure what came over me."

Poppy, still not completely over the fact the man had not believed her earlier, even suggesting she may need professional counseling, slapped the side of Jaxon's flushed face before allowing him to go back in for round two. With his next breath break, Jaxon quickly admitted he deserved Poppy's ire with accompanying flat hand. Her slap however did not seem to slow the display of his affection, but merely spur the unleashed emotion on. It felt like Jaxon was trying to kiss away all the pain in both of their lives in one sitting.

Poppy wondered if the respectable thing to do was to push Jaxon away, but realized she had absolutely no intention to. She had just found him, and he felt like home.

EPILOGUE

(just over nine months later)

It was Christmas Eve in St. Anthony City Park. The public relations person for the event suggested this date would be a moving and motivating time to hold the Open House. Not only would the spirit of the season lend to people opening their hearts, but also their pocket *books* (her play on words), better known as wallets.

A live nativity, including two wooly sheep and a tired looking donkey, was on display across from the decorated front doors. Placing Mary, Joseph and baby Jesus out in the cold, played to the *Inn's* theme. The name of the new edifice was scrawled across a large wooden beam above the entryway in metal script:

Bed & Book... Inn for Weary Wayfarers

The project had been placed on priority status and was completed in record time. Tonight was the Grand Opening. Some members of the library board had balked at the date, not only due to the rapid time table, but also the consideration that this holiday was a time for families. Jaxon had rigorously pointed out, what better gift could they give the community during this season? Those without a place to stay could come in out of the cold for Christmas, like their own families were able to do.

His observation appeared to be correct. The turnout was impressive. Being generous made people feel good, especially at Christmastime. Carolers sang in the background while families milled around sipping hot cider.

The structure was a simplified, abstract version of Poppy's butterfly-building vision. The right wing encased an annex of the public library stocked with six-thousand books, one-third as many as the main library. The left wing housed thirteen small private sleeping compartments which could hold two to three people, available for nightly use and up to thirty-day emergency stays. A second story loft could sleep an addition forty-eight people bunkbed style. No one was ever to be turned away at this Inn, if possible.

The live butterfly exhibit had not yet been delivered to the central connecting and welcoming area, due to the low temperatures of the night and size of the crowd going in and out. However, most of the winged beauties that had been preserved, those pinned and displayed, already hung artistically on the walls. A large glass encased corner was reserved for those yet to arrive.

Jaxon had insisted Poppy was the perfect person to be resident manager of the facility due to her double experience... both in library functioning and firsthand with homelessness. She was close enough to graduating with a library degree, that he was able to convince the board to give her a try. The main component or job description necessary for a manager of the Bed & Book, in Jaxon's opinion, was compassion and Poppy had that in spades.

There was a tiny live-in office space, a studio apartment of sorts, that went with the position. So ironically, Poppy would be back living in the park with the homeless. She adored the idea. Russell had agreed to be her number one volunteer, working there whenever his scheduled hours at the main library allowed. He and Xavier had returned from their travels and The Tigress was atypically supportive of the plan.

Poppy mingled with the attendees and was introduced to many who played a part in the venture. She saw Misty and Aporia were in attendance with Regina Bozeman as escort. Misty had been given supervised visitation rights with Aporia and was working towards a permanent reunion. Regular mental health and CSD appointments were part of the formula. Misty was surprisingly okay about sharing her butterfly room with the world and had requested to attend the unveiling. This fact indicated to Poppy that her former butterfly friend was on the right track. When Misty was deemed mentally ready, Poppy would have the discussion with her that she promised Bernie. Tonight, was not that time.

Xavier Max appeared and engulfed her in a squishy bear hug. He had returned from six months of travels a renewed man. There was even a little less of him to hug. "This is really something. I am honored to have played any part in it, even if it was just casting dollars your way."

"They say money is what makes the world go around, but I think it is the people willing to give it, in hopes of creating a better world, that really make the difference. Thanks again for your generosity Xavier." Poppy was happy to see her evolving friend. He really was a robust butterfly shedding his chrysalis.

"I also plan to pick up one or two volunteer shifts a week, so put me on the schedule. I can't let my new travel buddy outdo me." Xavier offered.

"Yes, Russell is an example to us all. I will add you first thing. Thanks again." Poppy gave the big guy another quick embrace before moving on. She had so many mentors to be grateful for.

Officer Platt was there in an official capacity and waved as she passed by. Mrs. Wentworth remembered her from the board party and had taken the time to gracefully whisper in Poppy's ear that from their first encounter she recognized Poppy had it in her to help accomplish something wonderful. Then she added with a chuckle, "I do miss the butterfly dress".

The Tigress even made an appearance, since the main library was closed for the holiday evening. Perhaps she was just checking out her competition, but for the first time in forever, Poppy saw a smile plastered on Moriah Bengal's stoic face. This place was going to make a difference. Joy was contagious.

She wished her Grandma Daisy and Chet could be in attendance too. Then a thought crossed her mind, how did she know they were not? A smile became permanently fixed to her face for the night as well.

Russell waved her over to the reception desk, where the to-be assigned staff would check out books and check in bodies. Poppy noticed a perky little blonde hovering there, draped across the desk making goo-goo eyes at Russell. Poppy thought she heard the blonde ask Russell if he would give her a 'ride on his wheels' sometime as she walked up. The girl was leaning in with her forearms on the counter top and being especially attentive to her Mr. Redmond. Poppy was wondering if the little tart had meant the wheels on Russell's truck or his chair. Russell was indeed a handsome man, it was inevitable he would attract interested women at some point. He couldn't stay cloistered in the library forever. The reality just gave Poppy a jolt. Blonde girl melted away as Poppy approached the counter.

"I need to ask for your permission boss. Can I leave out this volunteer sign-up sheet for the night? Sometimes dimes are easier to toss in than time and I thought we should strike while the iron or emotions are hot? I already had a person of the female persuasion here willing to sign up."

"Perfect idea Russell. And yes, that girl did look quite willing. Xavier said he would like to volunteer too. We can vet the names later. Thanks. I am so glad you are back." Poppy shared her smile with him.

"Yah me too. Did my absence make your heart grow any fonder?" Russell quipped.

"I don't think I could get any fonder of you Russell." Poppy replied.

"I see how the guy looks at you. If it couldn't be me, I'm glad you at least got one of the decent ones. But let him know I'll be watching. He better treat you well." Russell shared.

"Always my protective big brother." Poppy bent down and swallowed Russell in her arms. "We will make a good team here, Bro."

Russell laughed as Poppy moved on to resume her hostess duties.

The three hours flew by and the flow of bodies was beginning to disperse. She had not had time to really talk to Jaxon all evening. Poppy hoped he was pleased. When she finally saw him walking towards her, she could tell from his expression that he was. There was a glow in his eyes and a lilt in his step.

"We did it. We pulled it off. This place is going to be a humbly-magnificent addition to our community." Jaxon nearly shouted. "There is an additional project I need to talk to you about tonight too, Poppy."

"You are a driven man, Jaxon Cohen. The paint on this place is not even dry, shouldn't we wait at least until spring to talk about expanding?" Poppy asked. She felt his enthusiasm and energy but wanted to focus on Bed & Book right now.

"No, this project cannot wait. I have three acres of property on the edge of town that I am thinking about building a house and barn on. Not for horses, but an out-building with bunks. It could be used as extra housing for modern day hobos, you know, like those my grandma used to feed who would ride the rails, passing through town. Or perhaps it could house a woman's shelter. We can assess the needs of the community and go from there."

Poppy thought the man was playing with her now. "With a reading silo on the side or book barn access?" She added going along with Jaxon's jest.

"Poppy, I am serious. And I will eventually need someone to share and help me manage my new home, with an integral part of the property dedicated to housing those in need. We had the best matchmaker in two dimensions. I cannot argue with his choice." Jason continued to share his disjointed vision.

Poppy was not totally sure what Jaxon was alluding to, but she was getting trembly inside. Did he want her as a very green and poor business partner or was he asking for more? She did not want to read anything into his offer. "Let me get some experience here and when you are ready to open your next project, we can talk." Poppy answered businesslike.

"I am making a mess of this. One thing I did not inherit from my articulate father was his smooth speaking gene, especially when it comes to things of a personal nature." Jason took from his pocket a small wrapped package. "Merry Christmas Miss Poppy Paisley."

Poppy wished she had a gift for him in return as she pulled off the sparkly paper. Nestled in black velvet was a shiny single diamond surrounded by poppy petals. She gasped.

"It may seem sudden, but with all we have experienced together, our time has been magnified. I want to plant this Poppy, you, in my garden before you fly away. I have fallen in love with you." Jaxon waxed poetic. "You help me feel alive and to remember why we are here. Remembering and honoring those from the past is part of living in and appreciating the future. It makes life more-full. You expand me and give my life meaning."

"I suppose that is one reason we have history books. To help us remember and enhance our lives." Poppy, ever the librarian, interjected. Then realizing that was not the best answer, nor one a man pouring out his heart hoped for, added, "No one wants to live alone on an island of time."

Jaxon had not finished, "I am inviting you to share all time with me."

Poppy was totally caught off guard once again, but she had no instinct to fulfill Jaxon's concern of her flying away. She was not really sure how to respond, but unscripted words effortlessly floated from her mouth, "I would love to write our own storybook together C. Jaxon Cohen Jr…past, present and future."

Author's Notes

Did the reader have trouble identifying the antagonist? In this story the main antagonist is not a person, but Homelessness. Homelessness is a major villain and creator of chaos all over the world. Hand in hand with hunger, I could not imagine a scarier bad guy to work with. Unless I delved into the dark side, which I choose to avoid.

Nine cities in the United States are named St. Anthony. I did not want to pick a specific location for the setting of my story. Instead I wanted to make a point that homelessness affects all of us in every city across the country.

The nine months' time period, until the epilogue and creation of the envisioned project was completed, replicates the time it takes for human gestation and birth on earth.

This is my third book and all three of them deal with life across dimensions. I believe we experience communication from the 'other side' much more than we realize or perhaps accept. I also wanted to write about a meaningful issue. Although I have not experienced homelessness on a personal level, most people know someone who has. I have worked with refugees who spent their lives in a refugee camp in Uganda before arriving here (Vumilia, Moses, Joshua and Deborah). Those of us with homes, especially good ones…not in structure, but spirit and safety…are blessed.

My two main themes were glaringly obvious. Flowers grow where they are planted and can blossom in good or poor soil. Butterflies start out as a much less lovely form of life, but after they go through a confining time and space, become who they are meant to be and add beauty to the world. All of us are growing and changing wherever we are, much as the flowers and butterflies in this world.

Lastly, I have a grandson in a wheelchair who is as awesome as Russell, if not more so. He has much to offer the world…go get 'em Cash.

Thank you to any who take the time to read this analogical story. May you become all you were meant to be, wherever you dwell. Blessings, Teresa

Acknowledgments

The so-beautiful-I-framed-it, whimsical watercolor cover was painted by my daughter Chelsea Christensen Buttars. She captured and entwined perfectly the two themes of flowers and butterflies into one eye-pleasing medley.

Several friends and family members were willing to read various drafts and offer input. Teri Sowby, Julie Hales, Sandy Ostler, Angie Bledsoe, Brenda Mumford, Stephanie Platt, Lirenza Gillette and during an over forty-hour road trip across the country, I read the manuscript to a trapped Keegan Christensen who gave me great feedback.

I also wish to remember Mrs. DePaul, my first and best ever librarian at Harrison Elementary School. She opened my world to chapter books. I hope she was able to read (from heaven) the second grade note I left in her library desk drawer. I was not aware she had already left us.

Work Cited

https://www.huffingtonpost.com/bill-quigley/ten-facts-about-homelessn b 5977946.html

http://familypromise.org/homelessness-fact-sheet/

https://projecthome.org/about/facts-homelessness

http://www.greendoors.org/facts/general-data.php

https://en.wikipedia.org/wiki/Homelessness_in_the_United_States

https://list25.com/25-hard-to-swallow-facts-about-homelessness

Questions for Discussion

1) Have you ever been homeless or known someone personally that has? Do you believe homelessness is an issue? Is it being properly addressed in our country? In our world?

2) Do you think Poppy made the correct choice in using their funds for her grandmother's care? What would you have done if in her shoes? How did she handle her 'homeless' situation?

3) Did you think of Russell as handicapped when you were reading the book? What did you learn from Russell? Did you think he would be a better match for Poppy than Jaxon?

4) Was Xavier a likable character? Does living online affect interpersonal relationships with those standing right in front of us? What did he gain and lose from his gaming days?

5) Was Misty justified in protecting her daughter Aporia in the way she did? Can parents keep their children from repeating their same mistakes? Did you figure out Bernie was her mother?

6) Do you think Mona was really an angel of death or that it was all a misunderstanding? What are your feelings on euthanasia?

7) How was Jaxon affected by his father's homelessness and ensuing death? Did he rise above or wallow in the situation?

8) When did you realize Chet and Bernie were not still living? Did their presence in the park serve the purpose they intended? Have you ever had help from an unlikely source?

9) Did Poppy grow where she was planted? Did her flower ancestors give her a unique identity or assist her in any way?

10) What actors would you cast in the roles of Poppy, Grandma Daisy, Chet, Jaxon, Russell and Misty in the movie?

There is Love

By Teresa Meyerhoeffer Christensen

West Orion has returned to Hood River to wed his middle school crush, Olivia Tarkington. That is if he can keep her convinced for five measly more days, but then when does true love ever run smooth. Their wedding week is fraught with trials and tribulation…a broken arm, near drowning, heart attack, death and two shocking revelations. Will the besieged couple be deterred or hurdle their obstacles and make it to the altar (or flower-infused wooden arch)? This tale is introduced with wedding customs from around the world and then told through the eyes of the nineteen members of the wedding party as they move the story along to its culmination. Each person adds a different perspective on the events unfolding and amidst all the chaos…*There is Love.*

About the Author

Teresa Meyerhoeffer Christensen has experienced all the elements of romance, drama, comedy, intrigue, tragedy and adventure in over a half century of earth living. She was born in Idaho to a basketball-playing, college president father, and cheerleader mother, who taught her to love to learn. She married her high school sweetheart, graduated as an RN, survived cancer, raised six amazingly unique children, taught institute and seminary religion classes for years, was elected to the Bend-Lapine School Board while living in Oregon and served on various other boards in many volunteer positions, all while writing in various capacities. Life is much quieter now living up in Mountain Green and the veil between heaven and earth, along with the air, much thinner. She finally has time to put down on paper the many stories that have been roaming around her head for years. Teresa has currently completed three novels. William Shakespeare was her 12th great uncle.

www.teresameyerhoefferchristensen.com

www.ingramcontent.com/pod-product-compliance
Lightning Source LLC
Chambersburg PA
CBHW031709170626
46808CB00005B/1668